© 2011 by En

Library of Congress Cc

201190367.

ISBN-13: 978-1460941393

ISBN-10: 146094139X

I dedicate this novel to Mon Colonel – GIs who remained in France after D-day

May they rest in peace and honor for their sacrifice!

This novel is based on some historical facts. Historical fiction is a careful balance between fact and fiction and events may be exaggerated or completely made up for the sake of a good story.

Except for well-known historical facts, the characters, places, and events in this book are fictitious, and any resemblance to real persons, living or dead, is purely coincidental and not intended by the author.

Author's Biography

Raised in Flint, Michigan, Mr. Borka joined the USAF from 1955 to 1965 as a Cryptographic repairman. He participated in Operation Dominic, atomic testing on the Pacific atoll of Johnson Island, after which he returned to Washington D.C. and married a French citizen.

He was sent to France and accepted his honorable discharged there. He embarked on a career of managing technical writing and translation departments in European computer manufacturing companies. In 1974, he created and operated his own Technical communications company until retiring in 2006.

He lived four years in Holland and forty-four years in Paris and the Paris suburbs. Since retirement, Mr. Borka is actively engaged in writing fiction adventure novels based on French history and his personal adventures in Europe.

Works written by Emery Borka

Steve SANTA and the Secret of the Last PARFAIT

Steve SANTA and the BLACK NOBILITY

Steve SANTA and the ALCHEMIST BERRICHONNE

Steve SANTA and the Missing CHARLEMAGNE SQUAD

Steve SANTA and the CHOUANS

Bad Reichenhall

***

In the first days of May 1945, a patrol of twenty French Waffen SS of the Charlemagne Division surrendered to the US American Army. They were from the regiment "Hersche." Tired or injured, they were no longer able to fight. Along with other German prisoners, they were held in a barracks at Bad Reichenhall (former barracks of mountain troops). On May 6, 1945, the 2nd French Armored Division of Leclerc occupied the city. The French SS tried to escape for fear of reprisals.

They were finally captured in a small forest, encircled by two French companies. General Leclerc questioned them. When asked about their German uniforms, they replied, "And you, you have an American uniform!" Judging their attitude insolent, the general decided to execute them.

The execution took place, on May 9, 1945, near Karlstein, in a place called Kugbach. Told that they would have to be executed in the back, they refused. The Waffen SS French fell by groups of four, one after the other, shouting "Vive la France." The bodies were left on the spot, in accordance with the orders. They were finally buried three days after, by American military officers, and with names mentioned on the crosses.

On December 6, 1948, an investigation was opened at the request of the family of an executed soldier. June 2, 1949, the bodies of the SS were transferred to the community cemetery of Sankt Zeno, at Bad Reichenhall.

A few stories circulated about a 13th Waffen SS, who was the son of a French general, a friend of Leclerc, who have been spared the execution and sent back to his father. However, this was not confirmed.

Many former French Waffen SS, captured by the Soviet Army, died in POW camps. Those who made it back to France, including Fenet, were condemned to jail sentences for treason. Most were liberated in the early '50s. Unlike the Francs Gardes, they only fought the Soviet Army and, in the midst of the cold war, it was not real treason.

***

Steve Santa was aghast as he read this item on the Internet. Steve was an American living in Paris, and although he was retired, he worked occasionally as an investigative journalist for an American newspaper. At fifty-five, Steve had already lived in Paris for twenty-five years and was as Parisian as any of the French people living here. He knew all of the right places to eat, and those which were to be avoided.

Although he loved his profession, he had seen enough of computers to fill two lifetimes. His military service in the Air Force during the '60s as a cryptographic analyst for NSA had launched him into the data processing era with the speed of a lightning strike. Meeting a French woman in New York wound him up in France in one of the US bases in the east of France called Etain.

His stay in France had been fruitful because he learned French well enough to become an extremely fluent French-English translator. In his twenty-five years in France, Steve had absorbed enough French culture and history to be able to rival any Frenchman.

Steve met and married a Chinese woman Ping, who was a freelance interpreter. They met during the search for a Cathar treasure, which brought Steve to China and Ping became his interpreter.

Today, Steve was researching information on the Second World War and came across information concerning the 33èmc Waffcn SS Division.

This was a little known fact concerning Frenchmen who joined the German Army and who were formed into an Army division much the same as the Normandie-Niemen squadron who fought the Germans with the Russian Army.

Normandie-Niemen Squadron was a fighter squadron of the French Air Force. It served on the Eastern Front of the European Theatre of World War II with the 1st Air Army. The regiment was notable for being one of only two air combat units from an Allied western European country to participate on the Eastern Front during World War II, the other being the British No. 151 Wing RAF, and the only one to fight along the Soviets until the end of the war in Europe.

What was surprising to Steve was the fact that during his twenty-five years in France, he had never heard anyone speak about the SS Division Charlemagne.

— Ping, look at what I just found on the Internet. Steve asked his wife to take a look at the surprising information.

— You should take that up with the colonel this weekend when we are in Sacy for the mushroom hunt, Ping answered.

— You are right Ping, he was in the 2nd DB himself, and would certainly be able to tell me more on the subject, Steve concluded.

It was Thursday, and they were anticipating one of the year's greatest social events in Sacy. Sacy was a small village of 211 persons in the Yonne, which doubled most weekends, and especially for summer vacations, when the French evacuate Paris to spend time in their country homes. Sacy was only seventy-five miles from the center of Paris.

Steve's ex-family-in-law lived there, and he had the habit of going there for more than twenty years. He would take a room at the Moulin in Vermenton, a city about five miles from Sacy, but he and Ping would spend the day and most of the evening, and sometimes the night, in Sacy with some very close friends.

There were two important social events in Sacy. One was the mushroom hunt in August and the other was the Narcissus feast day, which was always the last weekend in July.

The mushroom hunt for Girolles and Ceps was generally in August, depending on the amount of sun and rain during the year. This was to be the next weekend, so Steve and Ping were excited to go. This would be Ping's first participation and general meeting of most of Steve's friends there.

Steve's old friends Sylvain and Michelle Barbier, owners of the Moulin, had reserved their room at the Moulin weeks ahead of time.

Friday afternoon, Ping and Steve put their bags in the car and off they were to Sacy. It was not only joyous to hunt mushrooms during this time of the season, but also a time when the entire group of close friends met to celebrate their friendship.

Everyone would meet at the colonel's house for an evening cocktail, which was inevitably a Kir (Chablis and blackcurrant liqueur).

After checking in at the Moulin in Vermenton, Steve and Ping left with Sylvain and Michelle to go to Sacy. They arrived to see that most of the friends were already in the old schoolhouse the colonel rented in Sacy.

Upon seeing Steve and Ping enter the living room, the colonel said with his forceful and commanding voice,

— Les Ricains (French slang for Americans) have arrived! We can start now; Genevieve, please see that everyone has his Kir, commanded the colonel.

— My good friends, here is to our lasting friendship, and us the colonel offered, porting the first of many toasts.

— If it is sunny tomorrow morning, early...around 7:00 a.m., I want everyone in the school courtyard for instructions...and do not forget your sacks this time Jean Michel, informed the colonel, who commanded the mushroom raid as if it was a military charge.

Everyone milled around greeting those who they had not seen for a while until someone said that Steve had not presented his new wife Ping.

6

— You are right my friends, and I will rectify this immediately, said Steve, taking Ping by the waist.

— I want you all to meet Ping. I met my beautiful wife on a mission to China looking for the translation of an extremely ancient language called Dongba. Ping is a professional translator/interpreter...Chinese to and from English...but she is also one of the few experts on the Dongba language. She went to Michigan State University. Ping works for many of the major conferences concerning Sino-American relations as well as numerous other international meetings. She is still learning to speak French so some leniency please, or try to use the English you all studied at some point or another, explained Steve.

Michelle chimed in with a warning.

— If any of you guys feel like getting fresh with this very beautiful Chinese woman, please note that she is a Wing-Chun master and I have seen her in action, Michelle concluded with a big grin.

Before the evening was over, Steve came over to the colonel to talk to him about what he had heard and seen about the 33ème Waffen SS Division Charlemagne and the incident at Bad Reichenhall.

The colonel gave Steve a stern look and became very serious.

— Steve, we will speak of this, but alone. I will not accept anyone else in a conversation on this subject. It is too sensitive to be treated lightly, even today, warned the colonel.

— Tomorrow afternoon, come and get me after we have our mushroom day. You and I will take a walk up behind the church to the two benches on the hill overlooking Sacy. We can talk calmly without being overheard or disturbed by anyone, the colonel instructed.

— Agreed, Mon Colonel, replied Steve, as he and the others called the colonel.

That evening, everyone went home in a joyous mood in anticipation of the next day's mushroom hunt.

The next morning, those going with the colonel were ready and waiting in front of the school with their sack. The colonel appeared and addressed them.

— My friends, from what I have found out from my neighbors, the best place to go today is the "Foret de la Nef" (the Nef Forest). It is only six miles or so from here and it is just outside of Joux-la-ville. We searched there a few years ago, the Colonel explained.

—   Remember, Girolles, Ceps, and Death Trumpet mushrooms. The Death Trumpet is a wild mushroom shaped like a trumpet. Its cap is thin and gently ruffled; its color ranges from dark gray to black. The flavor of this mushroom is rich, deep and somewhat nutty. Also called black chanterelle, horn of plenty, and trumpet of death, this mushroom can be found fresh starting in August, so let us go get them.

—   In any case, no one, absolutely no one, is to take any mushrooms from the sorting room until they have been verified to be sure that we have eliminated any poisonous mushrooms, is this perfectly clear to all? the colonel asked.

—   Oui, Mon Colonel, replied everyone in unison, just like every year before starting the hunt.

Off they went into the Nef Forest. When everyone had arrived, the colonel chose the groups to search together and their search zones. The first group was under command of the colonel's son-in-law, who had been under his orders when they were both military. They were eighteen men and women, so the colonel decided on the second group headed up by Serge, one of the group of friends who lived in Sacy and knew the forest like his hand. Steve and Ping were in this group. The colonel took the remainder of the people into his group.

— Remember to stay spread out and leave enough room between the groups to make the return sweep, the colonel instructed.

Searching occurred in a para-military manner under the commandment of the colonel; but they had all done this for years and loved it. It was a joyous moment and being deep in the forest was refreshing.

As they advanced, you could hear someone shouting from time to time that they had found a spread of Girolles or a Cep or two. The sacks filled up rapidly because it was a good year for Girolles. Three people even found a few Death Trumpet patches.

In late afternoon, they returned to the schoolhouse to unload their booty for sorting, and to eliminate the poisonous mushrooms picked by error. The local pharmacist from Vermenton oversaw the sorting. Everyone was tired, but joyful to get another Kir with crackers, peanuts, cheese morsels, and other bite-sized hors d'oeuvres prepared by the colonel's wife while they were away searching.

When the sorting was finished, some lingered on for a while at the schoolhouse, while others returned home to make the traditional mushroom dish.

Genevieve, the colonel's wife, prepared their traditional mushroom dish with Girolles, smoked bacon, and scrambled eggs. The colonel told Steve and

Ping to stay and eat with him and his family. Steve accepted with pleasure.

The colonel disappeared down the stairs to the cellar to get some wine. He came back with two bottles of Clos Vougeot 1959 and a bottle of Scotch.

— Steve, I have wanted to open this bottle of scotch for a while. It was given to me by General Maxwell Davenport Taylor commander of the 101st Airborne Division as a prize for capturing both Haguenau and Berghof just a few hours before the 101st. Who would it be more fitting to open this bottle with but my close American friend Steve? the colonel said.

— Mon Colonel, thanks for that. It will be a pleasure to share this bottle of scotch with you. It is an honored, Steve said.

Sylvain and Michelle had stayed to enjoy Genevieve's cooking, and later that evening, they took Steve and Ping back to the Moulin to get some well-earned shuteye.

The next morning, everyone slept in except Sylvain and Michelle, because of their responsibilities for their guests.

Freshly baked croissants made by the competent hands of Michelle were a wonderful delight at breakfast. They talked for a while about their adventure the day before, with the hotel guests wondering just what kind of feast they had attended.

The morning went fast. Steve advised Ping that he had a personal meeting with the colonel to discuss the surprising information he had found about the Charlemagne SS squad.

After lunch, where Michelle had out done herself by making cow's tongue with a sauce gribish, Steve left for Sacy at around two o'clock.

He went straight to the old school and found Genevieve making mushroom preserves, as she usually did. The colonel was sitting in a corner reading the local journal and smiled when he saw Steve arrive.

After all the traditional French hellos by kissing the air on the women's cheeks four times, the colonel took Steve by the arm and headed for the door, saying that they were going for a walk and did not want to be disturbed.

It only took a few steps to get to the church of Saint John Baptist, built in the twelfth century and still in use. At the end of the church, they turned left to go up the hill behind the church to a point overseeing almost all of Sacy. It was a pleasant afternoon and the sun was extending its warm rays over the area, making it a beautiful day to be outside.

When they reached the two cement benches, the colonel stopped and sat down, patting the place alongside of him for Steve to sit. After sitting for a moment and observing the village where he was born, the colonel started talking.

— Did you know Steve, Sacy is where I was born? he asked, without waiting for an answer. I love this little village and find peace and calm here, the colonel went on.

— Steve, I do not know how you obtained the information on the SS Charlemagne Division, but it is a somber part of the history of France. What I am going to tell you is very secret and only a few of us old veterans of the second world war know it and I doubt that there are many like me left to talk about it, the colonel explained, looking at Steve with a very stern look.

— It is true that during the war many different factions of the French population were incited to accomplish good and bad deeds. Some accomplished bad deeds while thinking that they were doing the right thing for France. Others fell under the spell of a criminal state that Petain created by surrendering the France to the Germans, he explained.

— Then there were the communists, who were the greatest resistance heroes during the war, and who deserve credit for their actions. On the contrary, others felt that it was necessary to combat communism with every means possible. This is one of the main reasons why a certain number of Frenchmen justified the fact that they joined the German Army—in order to combat the communist armies coming from Russia. There were about 7,340 at its peak in 1944, but the strength of the division fell to sixty men in May 1945.

— You know that I left France to join De Gaulle in England and enlisted in the Free French Army under his command. I was an enlisted man and was assigned to the 2nd Armored Division called the 2nd DB commanded by General Philippe Leclerc de Hautecloque, Maréchal de France. He was a colonel in 1940 when he was given command of the French Tchad armies.

— He was ordered to take command of the 2nd DB in 1943 and it became nicknamed the Leclerc Division. We did D-day in cooperation with General George Patton's 111 Army in order to liberate the French national territory. It was during our D-day action that I received a battlefield commission and became an officer, the colonel said proudly.

— We liberated Alencon and finally Paris on the twenty-fifth of August. We went on to liberate

Vittel, Baccarat, and Strasbourg, and finally wound up entering Germany and capturing Bad Reichenhall and Berghof, as you know, the colonel continued talking in such a way that one would think he was writing his war memoires.

— As you read, in May 1945, a patrol of twenty French Waffen SS of the Charlemagne Division surrendered to the US American Army from the "Hersche" regiment. They were tired and injured, and were not able to fight anymore. They were assembled with the German prisoners and were held in a barracks at Bad Reichenhall.

— The next day, the 2nd French Armored Division of Leclerc occupied the city. The French SS tried to escape, but were captured in a small forest by two French companies.

— I was there at that time, commanding one of the companies that captured them. The incidents following their capture are true and I still do not agree with General Leclerc for shooting these men. They should have at least had a trial. It was, however, legal in some way because we were under martial law in a war zone, explained the colonel with a heavy heart.

— However, Steve, here is the little, or even unknown, quirk of history known to only a few of us. Some of the men in the company guarding the captured French SS soldiers were apparently sympathetic to the ambiguous actions of these men.

— Before the incident with General Leclerc, the French soldiers guarding them allowed a squad of eight men to escape again. The French guards were not punished especially after the Leclerc shooting incident. The whole affair was off limits to talk about, the colonel explained.

— There were the group of French guards and eleven of us officers in General Leclerc's staff who know about the affair. Most likely, I would think that more than half of these men are dead now or would be very difficult to find, the colonel continued.

— The only thing we do know is that the group of fleeing French SS Charlemagne Divisions soldiers headed to Czechoslovakia where the German 7th Army controlled the sector.

— The 7th Army Chief of Staff, General-major Freiherr von Gersdorff, was witnessing the rapid disintegration of the German 7th Army, in May 1945, but I think some of the escaped French SS could have made it to west Czechoslovakia.

Steve had been quiet while listening to the actual historical facts recited by the colonel. He felt privileged to be one of the person's privy to this information.

— Mon Colonel, this is so very interesting to me personally because, as you know, some of us here in Sacy and Vermenton found a part of the SS war loot in the limestone quarries under the Château Aymeri le Marquis.

— You see this treasure was part of a treasure that was once in Stechovice, Czech Republic, and which has seemed to disappear from the face of the earth, Steve explained.

— We only recovered a part of this treasure in the limestone quarries. Where the rest of the treasure disappeared to no one knows, Steve continued.

— I have studied the Ratline and the escape of many SS and other Nazi criminals to Argentina, which is widely known now. However, I am wondering if the eight French SS Charlemagne Division escapees had something to do with the disappearance of the treasure from Stechovice. You know it is only one or two hundred miles from Bad Reichenhall to Stechovice, Steve explained

— I now know that a certain Colonel von Shaffer had redirected a part of the treasure from

Stechovice with the help of Otto Skorzeny to the Cravant limestone quarries and now I want to find out if the escapees were in on the treasure affair. If so, this means that the last part of the treasure must be in Argentina, where I am sure we will find the escapees, if they are still alive, concluded Steve.

— OK, Steve, you are the journalist, but I warn you that you will find blank walls and little or even no cooperation from any of the veterans because the subject is so sensitive, even today, warned the colonel. I know that you have already stepped on many of people's feet, but be extremely cautious about this subject in particular. It could put your life in danger.

— Mon Colonel, I will be very careful but I do want to carry out my search for the treasure to the end and find it if it still exists today, concluded Steve.

The colonel stood up, meaning their talk was finished. They went back down the hill, chatting like a father and son until they reached the schoolhouse. Steve took leave and returned to the Moulin in Vermenton.

When Steve arrived at the Moulin, Ping was in her room so he went right up to the room to tell her what he had discussed with the colonel.

— You know Steve; I think the colonel may have a point. You have done some dangerous things since I have known you. You are generous, but I think you must be more careful and avoid putting your head into the lion's mouth, Ping exclaimed.

— I know you are right my dear Ping, but you know that we only found a part of the Stechovice treasure. Somehow, I feel the responsibility of finishing the job. I do not like leaving loose ends like this, explained Steve.

— After all, I am an investigative journalist and it would make a terrific article in the newspaper I work for, continued Steve.

— Hey Steve, you are retired and only work part time for them, do not forget it, Ping insisted.

— Continually putting yourself in danger is one day going to turn out bad. You cannot always be as lucky as we have been until now, Ping warned and continued to insist that Steve calm his desire for adventure.

— But Ping, this is an extraordinary story in itself, not even considering the treasure. I wonder how many people are aware of this incident, Steve continued.

— OK, Steve, if it is just research here or in Paris, I can agree. However, if you leave the Paris area, I am going with you, Ping insisted.

— That is a deal my dear. Besides, I do not want to go places without you if I can help it. What is your up and coming schedule? Steve asked.

— I am preparing for another international monetary meeting for the G9, but it is not scheduled before quite a while, Ping answered.

— OK then I am going to start looking into the incident and see if there could be any links to the remainder of the treasure, and at the same time, I will write my article for the paper, Steve decided.

Steve started Googling Vichy, the Division Charlemagne, and many parallel subjects that came up in the search results. He learned that the imprisoned survivors of the Charlemagne Division were released years ago.

It would be helpful to talk with one or two of them to get an inside view of what had happened back in 1945.

Steve spoke French just like a Frenchman; but with an ever so slight English accent in the pronunciation of some words. Therefore he was readily accepted by French people much easier than most of his colleagues. They spoke French with such a thick accent that it was painful to carry on a conversation with them in French.

Steve searched out and found a survivor who was out of prison and leading a normal life in his own dealership selling cars. His name was Bertrand Grandville. He lived and worked in a city of the Paris suburbs called Émerainville. It was on the east side of Paris, only ten miles away.

Steve found his phone number in the telephone guide on the Internet, and gave him a ring. Steve explained the purpose of his visit was to investigate the incident in Bad Reichenhall in 1945. Steve did not talk about the Stechovice treasure at all.

That would be icing on the cake if he could bring Mr. Grandville to talk about the missing squad and their intentions. They made an appointment to talk over lunch in two days.

Steve said nothing about bringing Ping, but Ping would come with him to the meeting because Steve knew that she would be a distraction for Mr. Grandville, thereby, disturbing him from focusing too hard on what Steve was asking.

Besides, Ping was a very personable woman and was intelligent enough to participate in any kind of meeting whatsoever. She brought a plus into any conversation, and since she knew the subject, she could ask relevant questions.

They drove out to Émerainville to meet Mr. Grandville at the Lognes Émerainville aerodrome restaurant called "Le Briefing." The restaurant was located on the airport grounds, the largest private aircraft airport in the Paris region.

There was not a lot of traffic, but you could see the private planes landing and taking off from the restaurant.

Steve and Ping went into the restaurant and asked for Mr. Grandville. They went to a table where a man with a mustache was sitting. As they arrived at the table, he rose and greeted then in a formal manner.

After the introductions, he expressed his surprise at Ping's presence, but willingly accepted when he found out that Ping was Steve's wife.

They entered into some small talk about the weather and the airport until the waiter took their order. While waiting for their order to served, Steve started in with a question about the overall incident. Steve expressed his surprise at the little known incident, as it was a part of the history of France during the Second World War.

Mr. Grandville explained that because Steve was a foreigner, it was conceivable that he could not understand the French mentality concerning this incident, which was inscribed into a larger context of

Vichy, the General Petain, and the division between factions of the French people during the war.

Little did he know that Steve was perfectly aware of all these facts. Mr. Grandville had just taken Steve for another naive American living in ignorance of French culture and history.

— Monsieur Santa, you speak French rather well for an American. It is a pleasant surprise. Generally, Americans do not even make the effort to speak French, he explained.

— Mr. Grandville, I have been here for quite a while and I feel that it is necessary to adopt the language of a country that has given such a nice welcome to me, Steve replied.

— Today, I would just like to get your feelings about everything that was happening in May 1945 and your opinions about the decisions made and carried out at that time.

As they ate, Mr. Grandville launched into a long diatribe about the époque. He was very ironic and made a lot of satirical criticism of the events. Since Ping did not speak French that well, but understood it perfectly, from time to she would ask Steve a question so that he could repeat it in French to Mr. Grandville.

All in all the meal went well, in spite of the sensitive subject they were discussing. When they arrived at the coffee at the end of the meal, Steve launched into a discussion about that fact those eight men, or one squad, was missing and had escaped.

Steve noticed that this caught Mr. Grandville off guard and all he could do was answer Steve's question by relating what he knew about the escapees.

— Mr. Grandville, where could I find the list on names of the escapees? Steve asked suddenly and frankly.

— Mr. Santa, there can only be two places where you might find this list. One is in the records of the SS Charlemagne Division in Germany— if they still exist, and if you can gain access to them. Then, even if you have access to the entire list of members of the SS Charlemagne Division, it would not tell you who the escapees were. It would just be the entire list of men, he answered immediately.

— Another place where it might just be easier and better to look is the archives of the 2nd DB. You might be able to find reports dating May 1945 when the 2nd DB was in Bad Reichenhall, he concluded.

— That is all I can tell you Mr. and Mrs. Santa, except one thing. I know the name of one of the escapees. He came from the same city as I did back in those days. His name was Georges Ribbonet, he added.

In his opinion, one of the Free French Army soldiers was sympathetic to their situation or knew them before the war and just let them go. He hypothesized that they headed toward the German 7th Army in west Czechoslovakia.

His opinion was that even if the German 7th Army was disintegrating, there would have been enough opportunity to hook up with the Ratline or the Odessa operation and escape to a country outside of Europe.

Having finished their meal and Mr. Grandville having exhausted his knowledge of the incidents, Steve thanked him for his time and the information. Steve of course took the bill and Mr. Grandville left to return to his dealership in Émerainville on the other side of the airport.

Steve searched for the archives of the French Army and found two locations. One was in the Chateau de Vincennes on the outskirts of Paris while the other was in Chatellerault near the Futuroscope attraction park.

The History Department of Defense (HSD) is the center of the archives of the Ministry of Defense and the French armed forces. Decree 2005-36 on January 17, 2005, created it. This national service is linked to management of memory, heritage, and archives, one of the branches of the Secretariat General for Administration (SGA) of the Department of Defense.

The SHD includes the Historical Center Archives Vincennes, Archives Center armaments and the personnel of Chatellerault. In total, the second largest archive of France in size.

Steve immediately called and obtained a meeting with the French Defense Department's press relations department.

Since Steve was a practically unknown journalist, but he had credentials from one of the powerful American newspapers; he was received with courtesy at the ministry.

Steve explained that he was doing an article on the Second World War and needed to consult the historical data of the 2nd DB because of its important contribution to the liberation of France.

Impressed by the enthusiasm of the American journalist, and in view of Steve's rather broad knowledge of France and its culture and language; permission was granted for unlimited access to both the Chateau de Vincennes and Chatellerault.

Being an American still carried an aurora of respect from most French persons and this, coupled with fluent French and extensive knowledge of France and French culture, always opened doors for Steve with a surprising simplicity.

The Chateau de Vincennes was a stone's throw from one of Steve's favorite restaurants, la Chesnaie du Roy. The Paris subway would bring him directly to the front door of the Chateau de Vincennes, so the next day Steve was off to visit the archives of the Chateau.

He was especially welcomed because of the authorization paper given to him at the Ministry of Defense, giving him a somewhat VIP status. Steve asked to see the archives of the 2nd DB and a guide went with him to a reading room, where Steve waited for the young woman to return with a few boxes on a pushcart.

Hours of sifting through the boxes provided no answers to Steve's questions. He needed names of the 2nd DB soldiers in Bad Reichenhall on May 1945. Finding nothing helpful, Steve decided to contact Georges Ribbonet on the advice of Mr. Grandville.

Steve returned to the apartment and Ping could see that he was frustrated by not finding even the slightest clue concerning the Bad Reichenhall incident. Ping made him some jasmine tea and they talked for a while.

Ping had a way of pumping up Steve's moral when he felt low or discouraged.

Once re-energized, Steve was back on his PC to find the address of Georges Ribbonet, if he was still alive and had a telephone. One name and address came up in his search. The person was living near Strasbourg

What did we do before the Internet existed? It is hard to remember back to those days! Steve thought.

Steve called the telephone number he had found on the Internet, and it was answered by a woman's voice. Obviously, she was elderly, and Steve had a strenuous time making her understand that he wanted to talk with Georges Ribbonet.

Silence—then a hoarse and grumpy voice answered.

— Hello, my name is Steve Santa, I am an American journalist and I am writing an article for an American newspaper on the Bad Reichenhall incident, Steve announced.

— Since you are one of the few survivors of this incident, I would like to interview you to obtain firsthand information from someone who witnessed the events there, Steve explained

It took a lot of talking and coaxing to get the man to say yes. He would allow Steve to come to Obernai in Alsace where he lived, with the single and strict condition that any information given would never be linked to him as the source. They made an appointment for two days later.

Steve got on the phone again and reserved a room at the Mont Sainte Odile Convent in the mountains behind Obernai. Steve had been there before with friends on a long weekend and, although it had no stars, the Convent served very good meals, and their rooms were spotlessly clean.

—   You are coming with me, Ping, aren't you? Steve asked.

—   I was wondering if you would ask me or just go there and stay with a bunch of nuns all by yourself. Of course, I will come with you. I have never seen Alsace and this is the perfect occasion, replied Ping.

It was a 350-mile trip, so Steve bought tickets on the TGV (High Speed Train) to Strasbourg where they would pick up a car to drive the remaining twenty miles. By car it would take five hours to drive there, while on the TGV it was only a two-hour ride plus a half an hour to get to the convent.

The TGV ride was enjoyable and Steve noted that it was on this track that the French rail system had set the world record for a high-speed train at 574 kilometers an hour, or 357 miles an hour.

Although the normal train running between Paris and Strasbourg never attained these speeds, it was nevertheless like travelling at the speed of a bullet.

They arrived before noon and picked up the rented car. Steve drove directly to the convent, and did not even use his GPS to find it. They checked in, put their baggage in their room, and went to one of the five dining rooms where the nuns served the meals.

During their meal, Steve told Ping about the history of the Mont Sainte Odile Convent.

— Mont Sainte Odile is at the 2,500-foot-peak of the Vosges Mountains in Alsace in France. The mountain is named after Sainte Odile. It has a monastery/convent at its top called the Hohenburg Abbey, and it is notable for its stone fortifications called "the Pagan Wall." In 1992, it was the site of a terrible Airbus crash, Steve said.

— The mountain and its surroundings contain evidence of Celtic settlements. The mountain enters recorded history during the Roman times. The Vandals supposedly destroyed a fortress in 407. In the second half of the ninth century, when Vikings attacked the Low Countries, recently converted to Christianity and governed from Utrecht. The Utrecht bishops went into exile and stayed for a while here in Mont Sainte Odile, Steve continued.

— At least, since the nineteenth century, its beauty has been celebrated; the mountain, with the convent and pagan wall, is often included in tourist guides, he concluded.

— Steve, who was Sainte Odile, asked Ping.

— Sainte Odile of Alsace lived from 662 to 720 at Mont Sainte Odile. She is a saint venerated in the Roman Catholic Church, although according to the current liturgical calendar, her feast day—December 13—is not officially commemorated. She is the patroness of good eyesight.

— She was the daughter of Etichon (Athich), Duke of Alsace. She was born blind. Her father did not want her because she was a girl and blind, so her mother Bethswinda had her brought to Palma—perhaps present day Baume-les-Dames in Burgundy—where she was raised.

— When she was twelve, the itinerant bishop Saint Erhard of Regensburg was led, by an angel it was said, to Palma where he baptized her Odile—Sol Dei—whereupon she miraculously recovered her sight.

— Her younger brother Hughes had her brought home again, which enraged Etichon so much that he killed his son. Odile miraculously revived him, and left home again.

— She fled across the Rhine to a cave or cavern in one of two places—depending on the source—the Musbach Valley near Freiburg in Breisgau, Germany, or Arlesheim near Basel, Switzerland. In the cave, she hid from her father. When he tried to follow her, he was hurt by falling rocks and gave up.

— When Etichon fell ill, Odile returned to nurse him. He finally gave up resisting his headstrong daughter and founded the Augustine monastic community of Mont Sainte Odile in the Hochwald (Hohwald), Bas-Rhin, where Odile became abbess and where Etichon was later buried. Some years later, Odile was shown the site of Niedermünster at the foot of the mountain by Saint John the Baptist in a vision and founded a second monastery there, including a hospital.

— Here, the head and an arm of Saint Lazarus of Marseille were displayed, but were later transferred to Andlau. The buildings of the Niedermünster burned down in 1542, but the local well is still said to cure eye diseases.

— Sainte Odile died about 720 at the convent of Niedermünster. At the insistent prayers of her sisters, she came back to life, but after describing the beauties of the afterlife to them, she took communion all by herself and died again. She was buried at Sainte Odile Convent.

— Sainte Odile was made the Patron saint of Alsace in 1807 by pope Pius VII. The larkspur is linked to Sainte Odile as well, and is believed to cure eye diseases in popular medicine and superstition, Steve concluded.

— Wow, what a story. I wonder how much of it is true and how much is legend, Ping wondered out loud.

— Well, all I can say is that the Catholic Church has taken her very seriously, so I can only suppose that it must be true, answered Steve.

Steve started reviewing the questions he wanted to ask Mr. Ribbonet. Steve never used a cheat sheet when he was interviewing someone. He felt that it would seem like he was not familiar enough with his subject.

However, he also kept in mind the real questions he wanted to slip into the conversation. Those concerning the names of the other escapees and where would they have gone.

The following day, Steve and Ping went down the mountain to Obernai and straight to Mr. Ribbonet's house. Mrs. Ribbonet let them in and showed them into the living room where Mr. Ribbonet was sitting in a wheel chair.

— Mr. and Mrs. Santa, you are welcome here; please sit on the couch. Would you care for some tea? asked Mr. Ribbonet.

— Yes, please, Steve and Ping answered in unison.

— Before we discuss anything Mr. Santa, I would like to know why you are doing this research. What is your objective? Mr. Ribbonet asked.

— You are certainly aware that you will stir up some old muddy waters by looking into this subject, and I warn you right now that even today feelings among French people are still overheated about this subject. Some people think that we did right to go fight the Bolsheviks, even if did join the German Army.

— Others feel that we are traitors to our country, like the Marshal Petain and Laval, the Prime Minister under Petain. I am sure that it will take a generation or two to smooth over these disputes, Mr. Ribbonet. explained

— Since you have lived here for a long time, as you explained Mr. Santa, you should remember that a few elections back, France was divided into four distinct political parts. There was the extreme right with the Front National Party, then the right under the RPR Party, the left under the Socialist Party, and last but not least, the extreme left Communist Party.

— Fascism and Communism have not left the French political scene. Did you know that each of these four political parties received 25 percent of the presidential vote? Mr. Ribbonet continued.

— I have told you this entire prologue to our discussion so that you are aware of the situation here in France, and that political passions run very high here, Mr. Ribbonet concluded.

— Mr. Ribbonet, my purpose today is a study of events at the end of the Second World War concerning the French population, and more specifically the French soldiers. I am writing an article for an international American newspaper. Here is my press card to identify me as a journalist.

— I understand that you were in the 33rd SS Charlemagne Division at the end of the war. I do not question or judge your motivation. I am only interested in what happened from day to day, especially at Bad Reichenhall in May 1945, explained Steve, opening the discussion to the subject he was interested in.

Mr. Ribbonet went into a long diatribe about what he knew concerning what happened during that period. His story conformed to what Steve had learned about it, but he did not make any allusion to the escapees, the ones that really got away, although he did mention the first escape and that they were all captured again.

He spoke bitterly about the actions of General Philippe Leclerc de Hautecloque and especially about the fact that these soldiers were not treated with the minimum humane respect or in accordance with the Geneva conventions. Steve and Ping could feel the emotion in his voice as he described the events.

— In discussing these incidents with a family friend who was an officer of the 2nd DB and present in Bad Reichenhall, I know that eight of you escaped again and were never found until I found you. Would you please tell me the names of the other seven men who really escaped and where they went when they left Bad Reichenhall? Steve asked.

— Mr. Santa, these men are not accused of any crimes against humanity, and even the French government has pardoned and released from prison the others involved in these incidents. I feel free to tell you their names, but only on the condition that you tell me first why you want their names and what will you do with their names once you have them, Mr. Ribbonet answered.

— Mr. Ribbonet, I was involved with the recovery of a SS war treasure last year, but we only succeeded in finding one half off the treasure. In addition to being a journalist, I consider myself a citizen of the world. Since I was involved in finding half of the treasure, I want to find the other half and restore it to its rightful owners, Steve replied.

— I mean no harm or any action against these men and I will not even divulge their names in any way. I want to find them and recover the treasure because I believe they may have been involved in transporting it outside of Europe, Steve concluded.

— I believe you, Mr. Santa. We all came from Alsace. Their names are Heintz, Kaufmann, Köhler, Bischwiller, Haguenau, and Baysinger—all from Mulhouse—and Dammerskirch, who was from Heimsbrunn, a small suburb of Mulhouse. We all knew each other well, having gone to school together—except Dammerskirch. However, they all hung around together.

— Alsace and Lorraine are territories disputed between France and Germany. Today, Alsace and Lorraine are two separate, adjacent provinces in France. It was French until 1871, German until 1918, French until 1940, German until 1945, and French since then.

— It is obvious that the plan was to get to the German 7th Army controlled sector. We were sure that it made no sense to surrender again to the Americans because they would only turn us over to the French 2nd DB again, Mr. Ribbonet answered.

— Northeast was the only possible direction for us to go, he concluded.

— May I ask why you did not go with them? Steve asked.

— The simple but painful answer, Mr. Santa, is that as we were escaping, and already pretty far from the 2nd DB, I stepped on one of our own landmines. This is why you see me condemned to live in the wheelchair all my life, Mr. Ribbonet replied, with an extreme sadness and regret in his voice.

Steve and Ping thanked Mr. and Mrs. Ribbonet for their kindness and left. They drove back up the mountain to the Mont Sainte Odile Convent. They went straight to their room to talk over what they had learned.

Later, they went down to one of the five dining rooms where the nuns served the. They ate a healthy meal, but that is all Steve would say about it. Besides, the room and board in the Mont Sainte Odile Convent was more than reasonable. After the meal, they walked around the convent to see the sight of Obernai from a panoramic viewpoint; they also walked down to the Sainte Odile's spring.

Back in their room, Steve started telling Ping about a Nazi concentration camp not far from the convent. It was the only concentration camp in France.

Ping jumped on the opportunity to see what a concentration camp looked like, so they decided to drive over and have a look the next morning after breakfast.

It was a ten-mile drive to Schirmeck. Natzweiler-Struthof was a German concentration camp located in the Vosges Mountains, close to the Alsatian village of Natzwiller (German Natzweiler) in France, and the town of Schirmeck, about fifty kilometers south west from the city of Strasbourg.

When they arrived, they took the pamphlets available to visitors. Natzweiler-Struthof was the only concentration camp established by the Nazis on present-day French territory, though there were French-run temporary camps, such as the one at Drancy. At the time, the Alsace-Lorraine area in which it was established, had been annexed by Germany as an integral part of the German Reich, unlike other parts of France.

Natzweiler-Struthof was operational from May 21, 1941, until the beginning of September 1944, when the SS evacuated the camp into Dachau. Hans Hüttig oversaw its construction.

The camp was evacuated and sent on a "death march" in early September 1944, with only a small SS unit keeping the camp's operations. It was discovered and liberated by American Allies on November 23, 1944. It was the first concentration camp in Western Europe. Its system of sub-camps was listed in the "List of sub-camps of Natzweiler-Struthof" available to tourists.

The total number of prisoners reached an estimated fifty-two thousand over the three years, originating from various countries including Poland, the Soviet Union, the Netherlands, France, Germany, and Norway. The camp was specially set up for "Nacht und Nebel" (night and fog) prisoners—in most cases, people of the resistance movements.

They were to be eliminated by labor. They disappear without their relatives knowing their fate. The camp also held a crematorium and a gas chamber outside the main camp, which was not used for mass extermination; some Jews and Gypsies were murdered in it to provide "anatomical specimens" for the work of August Hirt at the medical school of Strasbourg University in Strasbourg, France.

Strenuous work, medical experiments, poor nutrition, and mistreatment by the SS guards resulted in an estimated twenty-five thousand deaths.

Among those who died there were four female SOE agents executed together on July 6, 1944: Diana Rowden, Vera Leigh, Andrée Borrel, and Sonya Olschanezky.

Since the female prisoner population in the camp was small, only seven SS women served in Natzweiler Struthof camp (compared to more than 600 SS men), and fifteen in the Natzweiler complex of sub-camps. The main duty of the female supervisors in Natzweiler was to guard the few women who came to the camp for medical experiments or execution.

The camp also trained several female guards who went to the Geisenheim and Geislingen sub-camps in western Germany. Among the inmates were also the Norwegian resistant Per Jacobsen, who died there, and Charles Delestraint, leader of the Armée Secrète, who died later in Dachau.

After their visit from the outside of the barbed wire fence of the enclosure, they went back to the car, somewhat shaken by what they had seen, even though the camp had been mostly disassembled and cleaned.

— You know, Steve...I cannot understand how men can do these things to other men. It gives me a horrible feeling looking at the place where they were tortured and killed, Ping said.

— I have seen news casts on TV about these camps in Germany, but it is not the same thing as being physically present before one of them, Ping lamented.

— I agree with you, Ping. Let us get away from here, Steve insisted.

They drove back to the convent and went up to their room to discuss what was to do next. The only Internet at the convent was a self-service machine in an open space with lots of visitors crowded around it. There was no sense trying, because they wanted to keep their subject as confidential as possible.

They planned to leave the next day anyway, so after the evening meal, they hit the sack early. The car trip to Strasbourg went quickly, and before they knew it, they were on the TGV, hurtling along at about two hundred miles per hour on their way to Paris.

Back in their Paris apartment, Steve was Googling to see what he could find about German military records, while Ping went out shopping for food. There was absolutely nothing to eat in the apartment except a few dry crackers and a few bottles of wine Steve liked.

Steve found that there was a World War II German military personnel service records center in Aachen and another records center in Berlin. However, it was obvious that most of the German World War II service records were destroyed during the war.

He wondered if it was better to search in France for each of the escapees. There was a better chance that he could find one who contacted his family well after the war. Therefore, he went on to PiPl and the French and German Internet telephone directories to gather as much information as he could.

While Ping was preparing their lunch, Steve began wondering, and finally got a gut feeling, that somehow the man from Heimsbrunn called Dammerskirch was not really part of the group from Mulhouse.

He felt that although they had enlisted in the Charlemagne SS Division together, he had not grown up with the others. This gave him the feeling that the man to look for first would be Mr. Dammerskirch from Heimsbrunn. It was, however, possible that he was living under an assumed name since the war.

Next Steve examined General Leclerc's liberation in the Alsace area on his way to Strasbourg, where there was a terrible fight to liberate it. The records show that the Germans had made Heimsbrunn one of the front line defenses to the south of Mulhouse. When General Leclerc arrived with the 2nd Armored Division, Heimsbrunn was shelled to the ground. No house was left standing, and many civilians were casualties. Steve then examined the death and burial records for Heimsbrunn.

He found seven members of the Dammerskirch family deceased at that time and no member of the Dammerskirch family living there now. Steve widened his search to all of France and could find not even one member of the Dammerskirch family in all of France.

Ping had lunch ready so Steve stopped surfing the Internet and sat down to one of Ping's delicious meals. They talked about what Steve had found up to that point. He had at least found out that Mr. Dammerskirch's first name was Kurt.

When lunch was finished, Ping and Steve decided take some time for to be together and go walking along the Seine River. It was a beautiful sunny day and perfect for an excursion afoot in one of the most romantic places of Paris.

They walked and talked, and sometimes sat on one of the cement benches close to the river, with Steve's arm around Ping so she cuddled close to him. After all, they could see young lovers everywhere down close to the river kissing and hugging. They wound up at Notre Dame Cathedral and decided to get some refreshments.

They were only a few minutes' walk to Steve's favorite café on the corner of Boulevard Sainte Michel and Boulevard Sainte Germaine. They sat in the back row of chairs, where Steve usually sat, and ordered something to drink. They sat there watching the Parisiennes and tourists go by.

When the sun went down, they decided to walk back to the apartment, as it was only a mile and a half from where they were, and both of them needed the exercise. Ping fixed a light supper and they turned in early because of all the exercise they had done during the day.

The next day, Steve got onto the Internet immediately after breakfast to continue his search for Mr. Kurt Dammerskirch, but this time in Germany.

— Steve Santa, I am beginning to believe that you love your old computer and Internet more than your little wife, who loves you so much. You didn't even give me a kiss this morning, said Ping, with a small and hurting voice.

Steve was surprised because he was so concentrated on his searching. He jumped up from his chair and ran over to Ping. Taking her into his arms very tenderly, he stroked the side of her face at her hairline just above her ear, which usually made her melt into him. After a sweet languorous kiss, Steve looked into her eyes and they exchanged thoughts with their eyes, not even needing to use words to know what the other was thinking at that exact moment. When Steve loosened his hold on Ping, he went back to his desk and computer.

— My dearest Ping, as compensation for my terrible behavior as your husband, I promise that tonight I will give you a foot massage you

45

will never forget, Steve said, with seriousness and a wink of his eye.

— Wow, Steve darling, I will not forget that; I will anticipate it all the rest of the day, said Ping, smiling.

With a smiling heart, Steve returned to his faithful laptop to continue his search for Mr. Kurt Dammerskirch in Germany, then in Austria. He found no one by that name in Germany, which was not so surprising because Mr. Dammerskirch's name had such a heavy Alsatian connotation to it.

Although the historical language of Alsace is Alsatian, a regional German language, most Alsatians spoke French, the official language of the country they have been a part on and off during the past three centuries.

In 1945, about 75 percent of the adult population, and probably less than 40 percent of the children, were fluent in Alsatian. There is, therefore, a substantial bilingual population in Alsace, as well as a universal Alsatian patriotic feeling among them.

Steve then started searching in Austria and found two names that were very close to Mr. Dammerskirch's name. One was a certain Mr. Dammers, living in Innsbruck, which was an internationally renowned winter sports center, and hosted the 1964 and 1976 Winter Olympics and the

1984 and 1988 Winter Paralympics. It would also be to host the first Winter Youth Olympics in 2012.

The second was Mr. Dannemarie, which seemed to have a French connotation to it; it sparked Steve's interest. It was especially suspicious because the man's first name was Kurt. This Mr. Kurt Dannemarie lived in Triesen, Liechtenstein.

Steve read that Triesen was the third largest of Liechtenstein's municipalities. It contained several historic churches dating from the fifteenth century. It also had a weaving mill from 1863 that was a historical monument. The population was around forty-six hundred.

Steve knew that a person in hiding would often change his name but would always keep some sort of their original identity, like keeping the first name but changing the last name to something similar.

Steve continued searching the Internet on the name Dammerskirch. He found that in 1016 the Alsatian town of Dannemarie is mentioned as Danamarachiricha meaning "Church of the Lady Mary."

Throughout history, the name changed several times and took on some French and German forms. The name in the local German language was Dammerskirch, Steve read.

Although Dannemarie is only about sixty miles from Heimsbrunn where he was born and raised, the similarity was too great. Steve felt that he had found his man, but there was only one way to find out. He had to go to Triesen, Liechtenstein, and confront the man.

— Ping, I think I have our Mr. Kurt Dammerskirch in Triesen, Liechtenstein. Are you coming with me on this trip? Steve asked.

— You can bet I am coming, Steve Darling, answered Ping with no hesitation.

Steve made reservations for the next day to go to the Saint Gallen-Altenrhein Airport in Altenrhein, Switzerland, because it was only twenty-five miles from Triesen. Steve reserved at the Hotel Restaurant Meierhof and a car at the airport.

Off they were again, moving toward events that they will not be able to control.

Triesen, Liechtenstein

Arriving in the center of Triesen, they could see the old houses were bordered by vineyards. Triesen, Liechtenstein, was also known as "Triesner Oberdorf." Traveling to Triesen, Liechtenstein, was very easy using the expressways. One could always visit the Triesen, Liechtenstein, tourist attractions while traveling in the nearby towns.

Steve and Ping checked in to the Hotel Restaurant Meierhof and went straight to their room. As he was tipping the bellhop, Steve asked if by any chance he knew Mr. Kurt Dannemarie.

The bellhop chuckled and replied, "Of course," he and everyone else in Triesen knew Mr. Kurt Dannemarie, "he is our mayor."

As the bellhop left, Steve looked at Ping and they both had the same idea. Either this was the wrong man or it would be difficult to approach him, and even if they could, it would be difficult to get him to admit his past.

— Faint heart never won fair lady, said Steve.

— What do you mean by that? Ping asked.

— That, my dear Ping is what my mother used to say when I wanted to accomplish something and was not adventurous enough to try to do it, replied Steve.

— This means that we are going to muster all of our courage and find a way to meet our Mr. Kurt Dannemarie, the mayor of Triesen, boasted Steve.

— But first, I am hungry and you know very well that what we got as an airline meal was horribly little and just as horribly tasting, exclaimed Steve

— Well for once, you are right about everything, my dear husband, agreed Ping.

As they both had a traditional Tyrol supper, Steve could not help describing the typical cuisine, one of his main interests in life.

— The cuisines of mountainous areas can sometimes seem shockingly high in fat and calories to those of us who work in well-heated environments and are too sedentary in our habits. However, the mountain people of past decades and centuries did not have such leisure.

— Living in some of Europe's most hostile and least food-productive terrain, they had to find and consume enough calories to keep themselves warm and keep working in the inescapable cold.

50

— Main dishes, side dishes, and desserts that come from the European Alpine regions will, therefore, routinely wind up emphasizing the use of calorie-rich fats such as lard, butter, and oil. The sweet and savory grosti of the Tyrolean area would be typical of this approach.

— The sugar-dusted grosti sec is very similar to other simple fried pastries in more northern and southern parts of Europe. In particular, sweet fried pastries like these, under many different names, have become traditional to eat during the Mardi Gras period.

— That would be when cooks observing the old "hard" Lenten fast would be hurrying to use up the fats and oils forbidden to an observant household during the time between Ash Wednesday and Easter.

— The savory grosti da patac are somewhat more unusual; they include riced or mashed potatoes in their dough. In mountainous regions like Val Gardena / the Grödnertal in northern Italy, they're usually served with sauerkraut in the wintertime, or—in summer—with fresh, briefly boiled cabbage or other vegetables, Steve concluded

— Dear Steve, you are an ambulant world cookbook, Ping exclaimed, with a teasing voice.

51

— My dear, it would be a shame after all my travels and the different countries I have lived in and visited that I would know nothing about cuisine, Steve replied in a purposefully snobbish-sounding voice.

They both retired early since the voyage was tiring and they had lots to do the next day.

When Steve woke up, he was careful not to disturb Ping. He knew that she liked to sleep as long as she could in the mornings.

Since the hotel had a Wi-Fi, he connected and started Googling the city of Triesen. There were many websites but most of them described touristic information.

When Ping woke up and got ready, they went down to breakfast early. They were pleasantly surprised that the breakfast buffet was lavishly furnished with fresh breads, different local varieties of cheese and sausage, and homemade jams.

There was a large selection of muesli, yogurts, various fruit juices, and fresh fruit, so Steve dug in and built up his energy for the day.

After breakfast, they went for a walk in the city. It was very clean and typical with chalets all over the place. On one side, there were sharply rising mountains, while on the other side there was the river and a long plain rising slowly up to high snow-capped mountains.

— Oh my God! Ping exclaimed, as if she had seen something terrible.

— What is the matter Ping? Steve asked, anxiously expecting something horrible.

— There is even a McDonalds here...look, she exclaimed with distaste.

— Do not do that, Ping. I do not know whether to be afraid or shocked, or even what to think when you talk like that, said Steve calmly with a big grin.

Back at their hotel room, Steve and Ping were talking over ways of meeting Kurt Dannemarie, the mayor of Triesen. The especially wanted to meet him on a personal basis, with no witnesses around to overhear their discussion. The information they would discuss with him would be embarrassing if he was the real Kurt Dammerskirch.

On the other hand, if he is the real Kurt Dammerskirch, he could have a violent reaction to the questions. They were treading on dangerous ground and they both knew it.

— The best way to go about it, Steve, is to catch him in some personal place, like home. We can use your American journalist card as a pretext to talk with him, but specify that it is of a personal nature and that is why we did not go through the mayor's office, Ping suggested.

— I have a feeling that you are right, Ping. Just go to his home and confront him where he feels the safest, Steve replied.

It was getting late and Steve checked the town hall schedule; there were no activities planned for that evening. He also looked up Kurt Dannemarie's home address. It was not very far, so they could walk over in a ten-minute walk.

It was after suppertime in Triesen, so they started out to see the mayor. When they arrived at the address, they saw a terrific looking chalet with four floors. They walked right up to the front door and rang the doorbell.

An elderly, but lovely looking woman came to open the door.

— I am Steve Santa, an American journalist and this is my wife, Ping. If possible, we would like to see Mr. Kurt Dannemarie, Steve said.

— Please come in and wait here in the alcove; you can sit on the bench while I go see if my husband can receive you, Mrs. Dannemarie replied.

After a few moments, she returned and motioned for them to follow her. They went down a long hallway to a door that opened into an office.

— American journalist huh? Please sit and tell me, what is your business here in Triesen? asked the mayor, sitting behind his immense desk littered with official papers.

— What journal do you work for, Mr. Santa? the mayor asked.

— Would you care for some tea or a tisane? Mrs. Dannemarie asked.

Ping replied in the affirmative and Mrs. Dannemarie disappeared down the long hallway. Steve felt that attacking straight off would catch him off balance and reduce his resistance to talk.

— Mr. Dannemarie, I have come to talk to you confidentially about a certain day in May of 1945. Please be reassured, I am not here to expose you at all, but I have a few questions about that period in time, Steve said.

Mr. Dannemarie turned three colors of red and Steve could see his blood pressure mounting, since he was a man with certain corpulence.

He started to defend himself by saying that his name was Kurt Dannemarie and he had no knowledge of anything in Germany in May 1945. That was a dead giveaway since Steve had not mentioned Germany in his question. *We have him,* thought Steve.

— Mr. Dannemarie, we know who you are, but we are not here to do you any harm or to say anything about you personally, Steve reassured him again.

— We know that you are Mr. Kurt Dammerskirch from Heimsbrunn and that you were a member of the SS Charlemagne Division and that you escaped with seven other members of the squad while you were captured by the 2nd Armored Division, explained Steve.

— It was not hard to find the relationship between the town of Dannemarie and its old German name Dammerskirch, Steve continued. What I want to know is what happened that day when you all escaped and where did the other six escapees of the squad go...and what did they do, Steve asked.

Just then, Mrs. Dannemarie came in with the tea and served everyone, then left. She had the habit over the years of leaving her husband alone to discuss business without her presence.

— I have the names of the members of the squad that escaped with you. They are Heintz, Kaufmann, Köhler, Bischwiller, Haguenau, and Baysinger. The eighth man was Mr. Ribbonet, Steve explained.

Mr. Dannemarie went into the same long diatribe about as Mr. Ribbonet concerning the happenings during that period. His story conformed to what Steve had learned about it, but he did not make any allusion to the escapees, the ones that really got away, although he did mention the first escape when they were all captured again.

He also spoke bitterly about the actions of General Philippe Leclerc de Hautecloque and especially the fact that these soldiers were not treated with the minimum humane respect or in accordance with the Geneva conventions—much the same as Mr. Ribbonet had done. Steve and Ping could feel the emotion in his voice as he talked on the subject.

— Mr. Santa, why do you want to stir up these old events, which have no meaning today and for which I am in no way in an illegal situation. It could just possibly bring a certain distain from some of the villagers, although I have served then faithfully for the past two decades, Mr. Dannemarie pleaded.

— Your name will remain confidential when I write my article. My preoccupation is what happened to the six other men of the missing squad, Steve reassured.

—   Please tell me what happened after you escaped the second time. Where did you go? Did you all stay together? Steve asked.

—   OK, if I have your word as a gentleman, that no names will ever be used or made known, I can agree to tell you what happened that night, Mr. Dannemarie said.

Mr. Dannemarie went on to explain that they had the complicity of one of the 2nd DB guards who came from their hometown.

After they got out of the stockade, they headed northeast where they knew that the German Army still had control. It was nighttime and they navigated as well as they could in those conditions, but unhappily, one of them, Ribbonet stepped on a personnel mine.

Although they stuck pretty much together, they had agreed that it was everyone for himself, and if anyone were injured, they would just have to leave him there.

They did what they could to stop the bleeding but quickly left the area since the blast of the mine would have been heard by the guards since they were not far enough away from the stockade.

—   The rest of us continued running by night and hiding by day, where ever we could find shelter. We scrounged food from where ever we could find some, and even stole garbage from some of the nearby farmhouses we passed.

— After about three days, we saw a German patrol from the 7th German Army. We were already in Czechoslovakia. The patrol took us to a city called Dobris, where an SS division was commanded by SS Colonel Baron Wilhelm von Shaffer. We were ordered to work with this colonel, moving crates from a train onto trucks near the city of Stechovice.

— We had the honor of meeting SS General Emil Klein and the famous Otto Skorzeny, who seemed to be responsible for the mission of taking care of the crates.

— One day, SS Colonel Baron Wilhelm von Shaffer ordered us to take a secret oath that we would never reveal what we were doing with the crates. Then he ordered us to take the remaining crates and load them onto an airplane for Otto Skorzeny.

— I could hear the two men talking while they were loading the crates. SS Colonel Baron Wilhelm von Shaffer said to Otto Skorzeny that he was happy that they had already hidden about a third of the treasure in France before D-day and that it would be in safety and ready for their return.

The mayor further explained that before the airplane took off. The seven men were sworn to secrecy again by making an oath of loyalty to Otto Skorzeny. However, only six of them were selected to go with Otto Skorzeny on the plane to an unknown destination.

Dammerskirch was not selected. He remained in Stechovice for a few days to help with a crate that was not shipped away. The next day, everyone, even SS Colonel Baron Wilhelm von Shaffer had disappeared from Stechovice, leaving him to guard the crate alone.

— Curiosity got the better of me and I opened the crate a little to see what it contained. To my great surprise, I found that it contained bars of gold, jewels, and some paintings, said Mr. Dannemarie.

— With everyone in the Stechovice camp gone, I knew that the Red Army was not far off and that I must get out of there as fast as I could, he continued.

— The painting was a Parisian street scene painted by Camille Pissarro. I took it out of its frame and rolled it up as carefully as I could. I found a tube recipient to protect it. Then I found a knapsack and placed the painting and as many gold bars as I could reasonably carry and headed out of there as fast as I could go.

— I finally found an abandoned motorcycle with gas and drove it until it ran out of gas. I headed southwest through Bavaria and wound up here in Liechtenstein, he concluded.

— How come you were not caught, asked Ping.

— That was the easy part. I found a US Army uniform, and since I speak French perfectly, anyone who stopped me thought that I was part of the Free French Army, he explained.

— I finally arrived in Vaduz, the capital, and settled in as best as I could. Everyone was looking the other way, so I had no problem converting my gold bars into cash in a bank account and I was even able to sell the painting for more than a million dollars, thanks to a business connection of my wife, he continued.

— I met my wife at the bank; she was from a rather rich family living in Triesen, toward the south of Liechtenstein. We married and moved to Triesen where I have made a new life for myself, he concluded.

— Mr. Santa, you can understand why I do not want to disturb or change the life I have made for myself here, Mr. Dannemarie said.

— Mr. Dannemarie, have you had any contact with the six other men since then? Steve asked.

Steve and Ping saw the man look to the left; they noticed his blood pressure rising again because of his reddening cheeks. They were sure that he was going to tell a lie, but they had no way to challenge his answer because the whereabouts of the six remaining men was still a mystery to be solved.

— No, Mr. Santa, I never heard from any of them since they left me to take off in the plane with Otto Skorzeny.

The man was ringing his hands and really starting to feel uncomfortable.

— I think I have answered all your questions, Mr. Santa. Now you must remember your promise not to make known what we have talked about this evening, Mr. Dannemarie concluded, as he stood up, indicating that the interview was over.

— Thank you so much for your enlightenment on this subject, Mr. Dannemarie. If you will excuse us now we will be off, Steve said, as he rose and started to leave with Ping.

Ping and Steve left, walking back to the hotel and discussing what they had heard. They agreed that most of what Mr. Dannemarie had told them was true and plausible. However, neither of them was convinced that Mr. Dannemarie did not have any contact with the other six men of the missing SS Charlemagne squad.

They ate a late supper and went back to their room. Steve searched the Internet to find information about this flight from Stechovice in May of 1945 or any information he could find on Otto Skorzeny.

Steve found out that, with German defeat inevitable, Skorzeny played an instrumental role in selecting and training recruits for a stay-behind Nazi organization, the Werwölfe (Werewolves), who would engage in guerrilla warfare against the occupying Allies.

However, Skorzeny quickly realized that the Werewolves were too few in number to become an effective fighting force and instead used them to set up the "ratlines," a secret underground railroad that helped leading Nazis escape after Germany's surrender.

Besides organizing the ratlines, which would form the basis of the supposed Odessa network after the war, Skorzeny was employed since August 1944 by high-ranking Nazis and German industrialists to hide money and documents. Some of these were buried in the mountains or dropped in the lakes of Bavaria while others were shipped overseas.

Skorzeny surrendered in late May 1945, feeling that he could be useful to the Americans in the forthcoming Cold War. He emerged from the woods near Salzburg, Austria, and surrendered to a lieutenant of the US 30th Infantry Regiment.

He was held as a prisoner of war for more than two years before being tried as a war criminal at the Dachau Trials in 1947 for allegedly violating the laws of war in the Battle of the Bulge.

He and officers of the Panzer Brigade 150 were charged with improperly using American uniforms to infiltrate American lines. Skorzeny was brought before a US military court in Dachau on August 18, 1947.

He and nine fellow officers of the 150th Panzer Brigade faced charges of improper use of military insignia, theft of US uniforms, and theft of Red Cross parcels from prisoners of war. The trial lasted over three weeks.

The charge of stealing Red Cross parcels was dropped for lack of evidence. Skorzeny admitted to ordering his men to wear American uniforms.

On the final day of the trial, September 9, Wing Commander F.F.E. Yeo-Thomas, recipient of the George Cross and the Croix de Guerre, and a former British Special Operations Executive agent, testified that he had worn German uniforms behind enemy lines.

Realizing that to convict Skorzeny could expose their own agent to the same charges; the tribunal acquitted the ten defendants, with the military tribunal drawing a distinction between using enemy uniforms during combat and for other purposes, including deception.

They could not prove that Skorzeny had given any orders to fight in a US uniform.

Using the cover names of Robert Steinbacher and Otto Steinbauer, and supported by either Nazi funds (or according to some sources Austrian Intelligence), he set up a secret organization named Die Spinne, which helped as many as six hundred former SS men escape from Germany to Spain, Argentina, Paraguay, Chile, Bolivia, and other countries.

As the years went by, Skorzeny and their network of collaborators gained enormous influence in Europe and Latin America. Skorzeny travelled between Franquist Spain and Argentina, where he acted as an advisor to President Juan Perón, with an aim to foster the growth of a fascist "Fourth Reich" centered in Latin America.

Absolutely nothing could be found about his mysterious flight in May 1945 just before surrendering. This meant to Steve and Ping, that the only source of information concerning the flight and the six other members of the squad was Mr. Dannemarie.

They would have to find a way to pursue Mr. Dannemarie, in order to obtain the information he knew.

They decided to move to a hotel in Altenrhein, Switzerland, near the airport. They would try to conduct their operations from there. Ping suggested blackmailing him because that would be the only way of getting the fox out of his hole. She cautioned that this could be a dangerous method, because when you have the fox with its back to the wall, it will generally attack.

They wrote a sinister letter threatening to expose him to his electors and cause a scandal that would make him loose his seat as mayor and all of his former prestige. Steve wrote the letter threatening to tell all if Mr. Dannemarie did not tell them where the other six men were or how he could contact them through the old methods like the Ratline or Odessa or even some more modern method like Die Spinne, which must certainly still be operational. Ping bought a throwaway cell phone to be used for communications should Mr. Dannemarie decide to communicate with them.

Steve drove back to Liechtenstein to mail the letter in Triesen to avoid disclosing their whereabouts. While Steve was gone, Ping went shopping for the small necessities to allow them to stay there a bit more since they did not know how much time it would take to crack Mr. Dannemarie and get the information.

Steve and Ping met back at the hotel and then decided to go out for a walk in the small Swiss town. Altenrhein was an airport located on the shores of Lake Constance.

Lake Constance is a lake on the Rhine at the northern foot of the Alps, and consists of three bodies of water: the Obersee ("upper lake"), the Untersee ("lower lake"), and a connecting stretch of the Rhine called the Seerhein.

The lake is situated in Germany, Switzerland, and Austria, near the Alps. Specifically, its shorelines lie in the German federal states of Bavaria and Baden-Württemberg, the Austrian federal state of Vorarlberg, and the Swiss cantons of Thurgau and Saint Gallen. The Rhine flows into it from the south following the Austro-Swiss frontier.

It was a pleasant place to stay and the view of the lake was splendid. The lake was thirty-five miles long and seven miles wide. *It was almost like looking at the ocean with the Alps behind you,* Steve thought.

Ping and Steve took their time and drove up into the mountains where they found wonderful places to walk and see the largest part of Lake Constance. They found an Alpine inn along the road where they could feast on the local cuisine.

Three days after Steve mailed the letter in Triesen, the phone rang. Steve and Ping were both jolted back to the reality of their mission; Steve answered the phone.

— What do you want? Money? You stupid Americans! were the first words Steve heard in the cell phone.

— You know perfectly well, what I want to know and I am determined to get it one way or another, Steve answered.

— All right, Mr. Santa. I will meet you at a Gasthaus called Alpe Gsohl. You must go to Hohenems; you will find street signs directing you up the mountain to the Gasthaus. We shall meet at two o'clock in the afternoon tomorrow, and I will tell you what you want to know, said Mr. Dannemarie, as if it was an order to be obeyed.

— I will be there; you can be sure...goodbye, said Steve, as he hung up abruptly to avoid giving Mr. Dannemarie a chance to say anything else.

Steve Googled Alpe Gsohl and Gasthaus and found that Alpe Gsohl was a rustic mountain cabin, which does without electricity. Therefore, it likely serves just a light snack. It had room for sixty people. From there, they would have a beautiful view of the Rhine

Valley—a spectacular view because one had a clear view of both Switzerland and Germany.

Steve and Ping were a little nervous that evening and talked about nothing but the meeting the next day. They tried to set up contingency plans if this happened or that happened, but of course, it was all futile because just about anything could happen.

After supper, they went back to their room, cuddled in front of the view, and listened to Rachmaninoff. They both appreciated a calm and smoothing music.

They just sat there for a few hours cuddled together not saying a word. There was no need to speak because all communication between them passed through their touching skin and the warmth they generated. It was one of those privileged moments in the life of a couple.

They were off to bed to get a good night's rest before the next day's activity, which they both felt could be dangerous...or maybe Mr. Dannemarie could submit to them like a lamb.

The next morning after breakfast, Steve was still Googling all he could find on Otto Skorzeny while Ping was making a few preparations. She went out for a few minutes to buy some things but was back in a flash.

They had an early lunch then jumped into the car and headed for Hohenems, Austria and Alpe Gsohl, which Steve had located visually on the Internet.

The drive up was a pleasant one and as they got higher, the more they could see of the city and beyond, and Lake Constance. As they approached the Gasthaus, they could see a patio with tables and chairs. The Gasthaus looked like a three floor Swiss chalet with a sloped roof that came right down to the ground.

Before they reached the Gasthaus, they passed by the ski lift. Below the patio, there was a large rubber playhouse for children, similar to what you see in the McDonalds' restaurants.

There was only one car parked to the side. Steve parked alongside of it. They got out of the car and went into the restaurant. The first thing they saw was Mr. Dannemarie sitting at the bar talking with the barman. They walked over to where Mr. Dannemarie was sitting and started talking.

— Mr. Santa, after all I have been through in my life, you do not think that I am going to let some puny American and his wife ruin everything I have built, Mr. Dannemarie said with a determined and angry voice.

Before Steve could say a word, Mr. Dannemarie pulled a pistol out of his pocket, pointed it at Steve,

70

and shot. Steve felt like a large cinder block had just hit his shoulder. He fell to the ground, but lost consciousness before his head hit the floor.

Automatically, Ping's Wing Chun training sprang into action. Using the Monkey attack, she disarmed Mr. Dannemarie in a flash before he even knew what had happened. A second attack by Ping sent Mr. Dannemarie sprawling on the floor unconscious.

Ping had just enough time to see out of the corner of her eye that the man behind the bar was bringing a rifle into action, but he never had a chance to aim it at Ping. She used the Eagle attack, which was fatal to the man. He fell behind the bar, dead before he hit the floor, with a broken spinal cord.

Ping looked at Steve and saw the blood oozing slowly out of his body. She started to move toward Steve when she saw a movement from Mr. Dannemarie; he was groping for the pistol that had fallen near him when he fell.

Again, Wing Chun had trained her to react instantaneously to any threat. She had studied the Hebei version of XingYiQuan, based on a twelve animal system in combination with the five basic elements.

In a flash, she was on Mr. Dannemarie's back with a special kind of headlock around his throat. She placed her fingers right in the pressure point spot that could cause immediate cardiac arrest.

— Now, you will tell me what I want to know or you are dead in one second, screamed Ping, in a high pitched voice with such a great anger that even the most dauntless man would hesitate to take any action.

— Quickly, tell me how can I find the other six members of the squad and where is the rest of the Stechovice treasure?

As Ping tightened her hold on Mr. Dannemarie's neck, he became frightened. All of this had happened so suddenly that he lost control of a situation in which he had thought he was the master.

— Follow the magic circle and you will find the men and the treasure, replied Mr. Dannemarie.

— What is the magic circle Mr. Dannemarie? Ping asked, tightening her hold a bit more, creating an unbearable pressure on the spinal cord and pressing her finger deeper into the fatal pressure point.

Trying to evaluate the situation and the position he was in with this little Chinese woman on top of his back, he felt that he could overpower her. He was a very strong man and he could have beaten Steve to a pulp if he had wanted to.

So he decided to act, which was his own fatal decision. He started to move to throw Ping off his back while reaching for the pistol. If he had known that Ping was a very experienced and highly trained Wing Chun master, he would have thought twice before he made any moves.

In the second after Mr. Dannemarie started his movement, Ping locked on the fatal pressure point in Mr. Dannemarie's neck and pushed with all her might.

Mr. Dannemarie did not die immediately but the pain was so great he could not move. Ping got up, moved the pistol away, and asked once more, what the magic circle was

— Nazca lines, he answered as his heart was giving away.

— Nazca lincs? Ping again asked, to be sure of what she had heard.

— Yes, Nazca lines, he confirmed as he expired.

Ping checked Mr. Dannemarie for a pulse; feeling none, she ran behind the bar to check the other man's pulse. Finding no pulse meant that he too was dead. She then ran to Steve's side.

Blood was still pumping out of his chest wound and there was a considerable amount of blood on the floor, so much that Steve began looking white.

Ping felt for his pulse and fount it, but it was very weak. She quickly called the 112 European standard emergency number.

When 112 answered, she related the facts and that an ambulance was needed very urgently, and the police as well. They told her to hold something over the chest wound and apply enough pressure to stop the bleeding. This was crucial. If his pulse stopped, she was to perform CPR on Steve until help arrived.

It took twenty-five minutes for the ambulance to arrive and take over the medical responsibility for Steve. The police arrived a second or two after the ambulance and two police officers and one female police officer in uniform entered the Gasthaus.

Ping started shaking and one of the medical team put a blanket around her to stop the effects of shock.

— Thank you...but how is my husband...will he live? Ping asked, with such a fear in her voice that the man from the ambulance reassured her that Steve would make it, but they had to get to the hospital immediately.

— What hospital are you taking him? Ping asked.

— We will take him directly to Krankenhaus Dornbirn, answered the man, as they lifted Steve onto the stretcher to roll him out to the waiting ambulance.

— I want to go with my husband, Ping said
    desperately.

— You will have to remain here with us just for
    the moment to explain what happened and
    why two men are dead and one is shot, the
    police officer answered.

Ping was almost ready to revolt and force her way
to go with Steve, but her force of character was able to
control her urge to be with Steve. She knew that many
answers had to be given to the police about what had
happened and why.

Ping told the story about the research they were
doing on the missing squad members and that they
had found two out of the eight escapees. Mr.
Dannemarie had invited them to meet him here in the
Gasthaus to talk more freely on the subject and they
hoped that they would find the rest of them.

She related the fact that right from the beginning,
Mr. Dannemarie shot Steve before he could even say
hello. She explained that she is a Wing Chun master
and how she used her skills to keep from being killed
herself and to protect Steve as best as she could.

However, she said nothing about the magic circle.
The police then told her that she would have to go to
the police station in Hohenems to make out an official
statement.

As the forensic personnel arrived, they said that they would take her directly to the Dornbirn hospital so she could be with her husband.

Ping was so nervous and anxious during the drive down the mountain to Dornbirn; she felt that Steve, her whole life, was slipping away. When they arrived at the hospital, she was taken to a waiting room outside the operating and recovery rooms.

She sat alone, patiently waiting for what seemed like hours before a doctor in his blue operating clothes came out and walked over to her.

— Mrs. Santa, your husband is in fine shape. He has lost a lot of blood but he will be on his feet and out of here in a few days, the doctor reassured her.

"Thank you, Doctor" was all Ping could stutter, as she felt the blackness engulfing her.

In fact, Ping was fainting as a backlash from the shock of the action that had just happened and the fear that she could lose Steve forever.

She woke up in a few seconds, and the doctor prescribed some medicine to calm her down and give her time to cope with the situation.

She saw that Steve was taken to the recovery room and she could see him through the little window in the door. Just then, a nurse came out, and Ping asked how soon she could be with her husband. The nurse said that Steve was coming out of the anesthetic and would be put in a room in about a half hour.

Ping waited patiently until a nurse came to her to bring her to the room where they had put Steve.

When she entered the room, she ran to Steve, held his head in her hands, and kissed him with tears running down her face.

— Ping, I made it; I am all right. I feel groggy, but the doctor told me that I will feel stiff and it will hurt for a few days. There was no major damage because the bullet just went into my flesh. It did not even hit a bone, Steve said.

— In any case my dearest Ping, I would never think of leaving you without saying goodbye, Steve chuckled, and then stopped because of the pain in his shoulder.

— Please tell me what happened, because everything after he shot me is a blank until I woke up here in the hospital, Steve asked.

— He must have felt very desperate to shoot without even a question or warning, said Steve

— You know, Steve that my Wing Chun training does not leave me any time to think, so I attacked Mr. Dannemarie immediately, which

77

disarmed him and then in a second attack, I knocked him down.

— Then I saw the man behind the bar starting to aim a rifle at me so I attacked and, unhappily, he died immediately with a broken spinal cord, Ping explained

— Then I looked at you and was frightened because you had lost a lot of blood, but my attention went to Mr. Dannemarie, who seemed to be moving toward his pistol, she continued.

— I quickly attacked him using a fatal pressure point. If I continued it causes immediate cardiac arrest, Ping went on.

— Then I asked him forcefully about the others in the squad and the Stechovice treasure. With no answer, I asked again while I applied more and more pressure until he told me that we had to "follow the magic circle."

— He then made a stupid move toward the pistol and I applied total force to the fatal pressure point. I asked for clarification and he only said, "Nazca lines," before his heart gave way, concluded Ping.

— My dear Ping, you saved my life. Those men attacked without warning so I understand that your training caused you to react immediately, Steve said to thank and console Ping.

— I think you will have to research what the magic circle can be. I have absolutely no idea what it could be, Ping exclaimed.

— Dear, I want you to rest now. I will come back to see you tomorrow morning first thing, Ping said, as she kissed Steve very tenderly.

The next day Ping was there at the start of visitor's hours and went to see Steve. Steve was sitting up in bed with a flock of nurses around him—they rarely, if ever, have an American patient.

An Austrian man in the room next to Steve's room poked his head in to see what the clamor was about. With the arrival of Ping, who went straight through the group of nurses and kissed Steve, the entire flock of nurses dispersed and returned to their duties.

— My God, Steve, I cannot leave you alone one night without you stirring up lots of female companions, Ping laughed.

— Hey, I am innocent. They just heard that an American patient was here and came to see me. The American charm you see, my dear Ping, Steve teased back at her.

— What did the doctor say this morning? Ping asked, hoping that the doctor would say that he could be discharged from the hospital.

— I can get out this afternoon after they change the bandages, but I must come back every day for a week to get my bandages changed, Steve said, grinning from ear to ear.

— Ping, would you please go to the hospital administration and see how the French social security and our complementary insurance will pay for all this. My medical ID cards are in my pocket in the cabinet over there, said Steve pointing to the closet on his side of the room.

— Yes dear, I will go immediately, Ping answered.

At the hospital administration office, Ping found out that Steve's French social security covered him because he was in the EU and the complementary insurance picked up the tab on the remainder, so there was nothing to pay.

Ping hung around in Steve's room until lunch. She had a complementary food trey as Steve's trey arrived. *They are very thoughtful in this hospital,* Ping thought. When the meal was finished, the nurse came in with a cart full of bandages and medical supplies and changed Steve's bandages. Ping had a chance to see the bullet wound, which was just a small hole in his flesh with purple to rose-colored circles around it.

Steve was then allowed to dress and he left with Ping, who had recovered their car from the Gasthaus. She drove Steve back to their hotel and took him up to their room. Steve just sat in a chair and gave a heavy sigh of relief that the worst was over, for now at least.

— Now at least we have a clue to finding the missing squad, and maybe the Stechovice treasure too, Steve said.

— You are doing absolutely nothing until you are feeling better. We are here in a beautiful place and we can take walks along the shore of Lake Constance. When you feel stronger, we can go up into the mountains, Ping ordered, in the manner of a strict nurse.

Two weeks went by before Steve was his old self again. However, the entire time he felt cooped up in his hotel room, he was on the Internet, Googling the magic circle with no result.

One day, Steve was about to give up when he thought of Remy Delaneuville, who was a specialist in Tectonics, the study of the earth's crust. He immediately shot off an email to him asking if the information they had gotten from Mr. Dannemarie meant anything to him.

Steve sent all that they knew. It, of course, had something to do with a location on the earth's surface, but Steve and Ping could not imagine anything it could possibly be.

Steve and Ping continued their walks and going to the hospital each day for the first week to get his bandages changed. Then Ping took over for the nurses and changed Steve's bandages each day. By the second week, Steve was feeling much better. At the last visit at the hospital, the doctor told him that he was OK...but the next time he should duck or hide!

They were now free to roam about anywhere, but Steve said that the best thing was to get back to the apartment in Paris. They had nothing more to do here in Austria or Liechtenstein, so they could operate better at home.

Back to Paris

Once home Steve got onto the Internet to try to find out what a magic circle could be, while Ping started preparing her next conference. Days of searching went by and Steve found nothing. However, he was feeling better and his bullet wound was almost completely healed. He only wore a large patch bandage to keep it away from the lint off his t-shirt.

The doctors in Austria had recommended that he go through a rehab program to be sure that his shoulder and arm were not affected in any permanent way. Ping had contacted the social security office to find an accredited rehab center close to their apartment.

Although Steve was in good health and trim, he was not muscular man. He was strong enough to defend himself in a fight, but as with most men, he had his limits. So working out in a rehab center was new to him. He was guided in certain exercises designed to rebuild strength in his arms and shoulders.

For two weeks after they returned to their apartment in Paris, Steve spent his mornings doing research on the Internet and his afternoons doing rehab. By the end of the second week, his general physical condition was taking on a new look and he was even developing muscles he did not know he had.

By this time, Steve was wondering if they had hit a dead end on the search for the missing SS Charlemagne squad members, and maybe even the Stechovice treasure.

As time went by, Steve started thinking more about the main personality of that period, Otto Skorzeny.

Perhaps he could find more information by investigating the cover names he used like, Robert Steinbacher and Otto Steinbauer. It could also be useful to study the secret organization named Die Spinne, which helped as many as six hundred former SS men escape from Germany to other countries.

Days went by without any results. Then, one day Steve and Ping decided to go for lunch along the Avenue des Champs Élysées, where there were many tourists and lots of hustle and bustle. The little sidewalk restaurants were filled with tourists and among them lots of Americans.

They had just ordered when Steve saw a man enter with his wife. The man saw Steve and headed over to their table. It was a man with whom he had done his rehab. They had talked a lot and sympathized while they underwent their exercises.

Steve invited the two to join them at their table and they accepted with pleasure. Everyone introduced himself. Once they had settled down and ordered their meal, the conversation started.

—   Georges, you never did tell me what you do in life. You know I am retired, but I dabble in journalism by writing articles from time to time for an American newspaper here in Paris, Steve said.

—   Well, Steve, I am a geologist specialized in the earth's tectonic plate movements, Georges replied.

—   Now that is what I call a profession. How did you ever get into that field? Steve asked.

—   Well I followed a scientific curriculum in school and when it came time to choose, I went to get a master's degree in geology at Arizona State University. I lived in Phoenix for six years. The last two I focused on my specialty field of tectonic plate movements, explained Georges.

—   This explains why you speak English so well, said Steve.

The meal and conversation were both interesting, and they remained at their table drinking espresso coffee for a while. Georges looked at his watch and excused his wife and himself because they had a meeting with family in a half hour. The couples exchanged phone numbers and addresses with the intention of meeting again. They had enjoyed each other's company.

Back at the apartment, Steve and Ping agreed that they had a good time and that meeting Georges and his wife was great.

— I do not think I have talked so much in a long time, exclaimed Steve.

— Dear, I can see that you do not know yourself. You are always talking to people all the time. You are the most convivial and interesting person I have ever met, Ping said, with a large grin.

— Well, it was a pleasant change from our work and searching the Internet and not finding any results, Steve said.

— Steve, I just got a flash. Georges said that he was a geologist right, Ping exclaimed, all of a sudden.

— Yes, he did, affirmed Steve.

— Then he might know what the magic circle of Nazca lines means, concluded Ping.

— Yes, Ping, you may be right. Every time I search Nazca lines, I come up with Maria Reiche's thirty-year study of the Nazca lines. This means nothing at all to me, said Steve.

Steve called Georges, but only talked to his wife, as George was attending an international geologist meeting in Tokyo and would be gone for a week. She promised to give him the message when he returned.

Steve returned to the Internet to study more about Otto Skorzeny's post-war organization. Die Spinne, translated as "The Spider," was the leading post-war SS organization led (in part) by Otto Skorzeny, Hitler's commando chief, as well as Nazi intelligence officer Reinhard Gehlen, who was later instrumental in the formation of the post-war German intelligence agency, the BND (Bundesnachrichtendienst).

The International Military Tribunal at Nuremberg branded the SS, which supplied members and resources for Die Spinne after World War II, as an "army of outlaws" reflecting the cruel and opportunistic nature of the Nazi Party and its political and military operations.

According to Mr. Infield, the idea for the Die Spinne network had actually begun in 1944 as Hitler's chief intelligence officer, Reinhard Gehlen, foresaw a possible downfall of the Third Reich due to Nazi military failures in Russia. T.H. Tetens, expert on German geopolitics and member of the US War Crimes Commission in 1946 and 1947, referred to a group overlapping with Die Spinne as the Führungsring "a kind of political Mafia, with headquarters in Madrid...serving various purposes"

During the period from 1945 to 1950, Die Spinne leader Skorzeny facilitated the escape of Nazi war criminals from war-criminal prisons to Memmingen, Bavaria, through Austria and Switzerland into Italy. The skillful and well-planned escapes were unnoticed by many US military personnel; although certain US military authorities supposedly knew and took no action.

The central European headquarters of Die Spinne as of 1948 was in Gmunden, Austria. A coordinating office for international Die Spinne operations in Madrid, Spain, by Otto Skorzeny, under the control of Generalissimo Francisco Franco, whose victory in the Spanish Civil War was guaranteed by economic and military support from Hitler and Mussolini.

When a Die Spinne Nazi delegation visited Madrid in 1959, Franco stated, "Please regard Spain as your second Fatherland." Skorzeny used the resources of Die Spinne to allow Nazi concentration camp "doctor," Joseph Mengele, conductor of innumerable torturous "medical experiments" to escape to Argentina in 1949.

Die Spinne leader, Skorzeny, requested the assistance of ultra-wealthy German industrialist Alfried Krupp, whose company controlled 138 private concentration camps under the Third Reich, which was granted in 1951. Skorzeny became Krupp's representative in industrial business ventures in Argentina; a country harbored a strong pro-Nazi political element throughout World War II and afterward, regardless of a nominal declaration of loyalty to the Allies as World War II ended.

It was in Argentina, Chile, Paraguay, and Peru that Die Spinne became most influential in the Western Hemisphere by the early 1980s, with the help of Die Spinne leaders in Spain, with ties involving Paraguayan dictator Alfredo Stroessner.

War Crimes investigator Simon Wiesenthal claimed that Joseph Mengele had stayed at the notorious Colonia Dignidad Nazi colony in Chile in 1979, and finally lived in Paraguay until his death.

As of the early 1980s, Die Spinne's Mengele was advising Stroessner's ethnic German Paraguayan police on how to reduce native Paraguayan Indians in the Chaco Region to slave labor.

A wealthy and powerful post-World-War-II underground Nazi political contingent held sway in Argentina as of the late 1960s, which included many ethnic German Nazi immigrants and their descendants.

Steve was surprised at what he had found. No one had ever talked about this, even back in the '40s and '50s when it was happening. It was vaguely known, that some Nazis had taken refuge in Argentina and a few other South American countries after the war.

Now Steve had to decide if he was to follow the lead that would most certainly lead him to the missing SS Charlemagne squad and maybe the Stechovice treasure too.

However, his experience with Mr. Dannemarie in Austria was an important warning that he should not take lightly any decision to pursue this course of action. He could be putting his life at stake and maybe that of Ping as well.

Steve discussed what he had found with Ping and they decided together that it was best to wait until Georges was back in Paris to see what he could tell them about the magic circle, before deciding what to do.

The rest of the week went by quickly and, one day, the phone rang; it was George, who was back in Paris. He would be glad to try to help them solve the problem of the magic circle. They decided to meet the next day at Georges' apartment because all of his technical material was there, and it might be helpful to solve the riddle of the magic circle.

— Steve, what is this story about a magic circle of the Nazca lines, asked Georges, after they were settled into Georges' office.

— This is all we know, said Ping, after relating the whole story about Mr. Dannemarie.

— Let me give you quick review of geography, said Georges.

— In geography, the latitude of a location on the earth is the angular distance of that location north or south of the equator. The latitude is an angle, and is measured in degrees.

— The equator has latitude of 0°, the North Pole has latitude of 90° north, and the South Pole has latitude of 90° south. Together, latitude and longitude is used as a geographic coordinate system to specify any location on the globe, explained Georges.

— So apparently, this problem seems to be a circle that has something to do with the Nazca lines, but they are simple lines or geometric shapes; more than seventy are designs of animals, birds, fish, or human figures.

— The largest figures are over two hundred meters across. Scholars differ in interpreting the purpose of the designs, but they generally ascribe religious significance to them, Georges continued.

— The geometric ones could indicate the flow of water or were linked to rituals to summon water. The spiders, birds, and plants could be fertility symbols. Other possible explanations include irrigation schemes or giant astronomical calendars, he concluded.

— I do not see how they can identify a specific location, Steve asked.

— Steve these were discovered by Maria Reiche, a German-born mathematician and archaeologist who was famous for her research in the Nazca lines in Peru, beginning in 1940. These are not the only lines she studied. There are also global lines that circle the earth showing the alignment of certain ancient sites such as Easter Island, Fatima, Rome, Siwa, Giza, Luxor, Mecca, and Mohenjo-Daro, Georges went on.

— How many of these ancient sites are in South America and especially Argentina, asked Steve on the hunch that the Nazis took the Stechovice treasure with them.

— Let me see, said Georges, while searching for a book in his library.

— There are effectively three in South America, depending on the circle you use, and I am looking at the Nazca circles. These are Paratoari, Peru; Ollantaytambo, Peru; and Nazca, Peru. So if you are looking for something it should be located near these sites, Georges concluded.

Steve and Ping left after thanking Georges for his help. They returned to the apartment and Steve started Googling the three cities and Maria Reiche to see what information he could gather.

All he could find concerning Maria Reiche was that she was born May 15, 1903 in Dresden. She studied mathematics, geography, and languages at the Dresden Technical University.

In 1932, she began work as a nanny and teacher for the children of a German consul in Cuzco, Peru. In 1934, she lost one of her fingers to gangrene. The same year she became a teacher in Lima and did scientific translations.

When World War II broke out, she decided not to return to Germany. She did not seem to be a Nazi sympathizer—so he could not connect her to the SS who fled Europe by going to South America.

By Googling Paratoari, Steve found that it was known as the Pyramids of Paratoari, Pyramids of Pantiacolla, or "The Dots" and that it was a site within southeast Peru's Manu area of dense tropical rainforests, composed of pyramid-shaped formations. It was first identified via a NASA satellite photograph number C-S11-32W071-03, released in 1976.

They subsequently garnered greater attention among South America aficionados through a series of three articles, which questioned from afar what "The Dots" might truly represent, and settled upon a geological explanation being the most plausible in the 1977 to 1979 issues of the *South American Explorer* journal.

Ollantaytambo turned out to be a town and an Inca archaeological site in southern Peru some sixty kilometers northwest of the city of Cusco.

It is located at an altitude of 2,792 meters (9,160 feet) above sea level in the district of Ollantaytambo, province of Urubamba, Cusco region.

During the Inca Empire, Ollantaytambo was the royal estate of Emperor Pachacuti, who conquered the region and built the town and a ceremonial center. At the time of the Spanish conquest of Peru, it served as a stronghold for Manco Inca Yupanqui, leader of the Inca resistance.

Nowadays, it is an important tourist attraction because of its Inca buildings and as one of the most common starting points for the three-day, four-night hike known as the "Inca Trail."

Nazca is the site of the Nazca lines, which are a series of ancient geoglyphs located in the Nazca Desert in southern Peru.

They were designated a UNESCO World Heritage Site in 1994. The high, arid plateau stretches more than fifty miles between the towns of Nazca and Palpa on the Pampas de Jumana, about 250 miles south of Lima.

Although some local geoglyphs resemble Paracas motifs, scholars believe the Nazca Lines were created by the Nazca culture between 400 and 650 AD.

The hundreds of individual figures range in complexity from simple lines to stylized hummingbirds, spiders, monkeys, fish, sharks, orcas, llamas, and lizards.

The lines are shallow designs made in the ground by removing the ubiquitous reddish pebbles and uncovering the whitish ground beneath.

The largest figures are over 660 feet across. Scholars differ in interpreting the purpose of the designs, but they generally ascribe religious significance to them.

Why in the world would the escaping Nazis go here to hide the treasure that would supposedly help them to create the Fourth Reich? Steve wondered.

Steve did notice something that seemed to be a bit odd concerning Maria Riche. It was indicated that she wanted to prescrvc the Nazca lines from encroaching traffic—the area is near the Pan American Highway—and various government schemes. Reiche spent considerable money in her efforts in lobbying and education.

She convinced the government to restrict public access to the area. She sponsored construction of a tower near the highway so that visitors could have an overview of the lines.

Just where did she find a source for the considerable amount of money she invested in the effort to lobby and educate people about the Nazca lines.

Since she worked as a nanny and teacher for the children of a German consul, she could not have a personal fortune. Therefore, the money came from another source and the only thing that Steve could find is the Nazis Stechovice treasure.

Steve remembered that Skorzeny became Krupp's representative in industrial business ventures in South America. He found that they had offices in Lima, Peru, as well.

All the information Steve could find seemed to be converging to one place—Peru—and it could be any of the three places on the Nazca line that would be the place to locate the treasure and its guardians, the escaped SS personnel that fled Europe on the Ratline.

With all of the clues pointing to Peru, Steve and Ping discussed the opportunity to go there and see what they could find. The decision should not be made lightly, considering what had happened in Austria and Liechtenstein.

Ping felt that Steve had not recovered enough from his gunshot wound, but Steve felt that he was OK since it had happened more than a couple of weeks ago. They finally agreed and Steve got onto the Internet to find a flight and hotels in Peru and the trip to Cuzco. They would leave in two weeks, after getting the necessary reservations.

Peru

Steve booked a flight on TAM Brazilian Airlines. They had to leave Paris at 8:00 p.m. with a change in Rio de Janeiro, and the entire flight took 19.5 hours.

Lima is the capital and largest city of Peru. It is located in the valleys of the Chillón, Rímac, and Lurín Rivers, in the central part of the country, on a desert coast overlooking the Pacific Ocean.

Together with the seaport of Callao, it forms a contiguous urban area known as the Lima Metropolitan Area. With a population fast approaching nine million, Lima is the fifth largest city in Latin America. Lima is home to one of the largest financial centers in Latin America

Spanish conquistador Francisco Pizarro founded Lima on January 18, 1535, as La Ciudad de los Reyes, or "The City of Kings." It became the capital and most important city in the Spanish Viceroyalty of Peru.

Following the Peruvian War of Independence, it became the capital of the Republic of Peru. Today, around one-third of the Peruvian population lives in the metropolitan area.

Steve had reserved at the JW Marriott Hotel Lima, which had a superb location, awe-inspiring architecture, and magnificent views. Standing in front of the grand cliffs in the Miraflores district, the JW Marriott luxury hotel in Lima offered sweeping views of the Pacific Ocean from every guest room.

The hotel's twenty-five-story, ultra-modern glass tower made it one of the best Lima hotels. The JW Marriott Hotel Lima was home to a five-star gourmet restaurant, which Steve and Ping would enjoy.

They only spent two days in Lima, the time needed to recover from the flight and organize how they would get to Cuzco and reserve a hotel room. Steve found a flight on the Star Peru Airline that would take them to the Aeropuerto Velasco Astete in Cuzco. He also reserved their hotel room at the Boutique Hotel, Andean Wings.

The Andean Wings Hotel is a charming and majestic hotel where there is a perfect mixture of style, harmony and top-of-the-art.

Located in a reconditioned old, colonial house, which has over three hundred years of history, it lies just over two blocks away from the historical center plaza of Cuzco, the true heart of the Peruvian Andes.

The hotel provided all the commodities of a five-star hotel, combining them with the modern concept of boutique hotel, which delighted Steve and Ping. They had one of the fourteen rooms, which was carefully and originally decorated, designed, and implemented.

It included a sophisticated Jacuzzi and a well-sorted frigo-bar.

One could purchase every piece of furniture, such as candlelights, paintings, chairs and tables, cabinets, was an old Peruvian antiquity.

Once they had arrived in Cuzco and checked in, they went to their room and unpacked. Then Steve started looking for transportation. He found a Toyota multi-terrain, 4Runner Trail at a Hertz office.

Meanwhile Ping had gone down to buy maps of the area and a handheld GPS device to be able to navigate correctly in a country where neither of them had set foot and where neither of them spoke the local language, Spanish.

They began to plot a course to visit the three cities found along the magic circle—Paratoari, Ollantaytambo, and Nazca.

Ollantaytambo was about fifty-six miles through very rugged mountainous terrain. It would take about one and a half hours to drive there.

Nazca was five hundred miles away and it would take more than ten hours to get there, and through even more rugged mountainous terrain.

On the other hand, Steve found that Paratoari was very difficult to get there. It was in the Manu Rainforest and Wildlife Park. Manu, located in the southeast area of Peru, is one of the largest parks in South America.

The area of the park encompassed parts of the Andean department of Cuzco and the jungle department of Madre de Dios. All Steve could find for Paratoari was its GPS location 12° 40' 23.39' S, 71° 27' 40.32' W.

All Manu trips started and ended in Cusco and included all air and ground transport, food, lodging, and guided rainforest outings. The InkaNatura tourist company used the highly maneuverable, versatile, and well-equipped twin otter.

The twin otter was a high-winged and twin-engine turboprop aircraft carrying passengers between Cusco and Boca Manu, the airstrip in Manu area.

The Amazon rainforest is the largest tropical forest on Earth, covering about 2.7 million square miles (seven million square kilometers) or 90 percent the size of the forty-eight lower states of the U.S.

Though the Peruvian Amazon is only 10 percent of this total, it represents the wildest, most wildlife-packed rainforest in the world.

This led Steve and Ping to save this site for the last if the others gave no results.

They finally decided to go to Ollantaytambo first because it was only fifty miles away.

While they were eating dinner, Ping told Steve that since they were there, they must absolutely visit Machu Picchu after they had finished in Ollantaytambo, because Aguas Calientes was only twenty miles further on the same road.

— Steve, it would be a shame to be so close and not go there to see one of the greatest Inca cities, Ping said when she saw Steve's face close up as she spoke.

— OK Ping, but remember what we are here for. I agree that it would be silly to miss it, Steve agreed.

After a good night's sleep, they were up and ready to go at dawn. They put a small bag into the 4Runner Trail and off they were on the road to Ollantaytambo. The route was a variation of lush green pastures with rolling hills and mountains always in the background. Although they were about nine thousand feet above sea level, they were surprised to see the clouds rolling over and hugging the contours of the hills.

They saw as many plowed fields as terraced plantations. It was surprising how much farming there was in this area, but it was such beautiful scenery to enjoy on their trip. They passed a few whistle-stop villages as well as one larger city called Chinchero.

Leaving Chinchero, they drove until they could have a look at the agricultural terraces of Moray as well as the saltpans of Maras. Moray was an agricultural terrace complex northwest of Cuzco, south of the Sacred Valley.

It might make some people think of UFOs or crop circles, or volcano craters, but this site was just a manmade agricultural complex. Therefore, it had more to do with potatoes than aliens did do. Moray was harder to access than most other places in the region, therefore, fewer people visit it.

There were not large crowds, so it was easier to take good pictures with their camera, without waiting for the crowds to move away.

Ping pointed out that Moray resembles ancient Greek and Roman amphitheaters and when sighted, the traveler might feel elevated, impressed of the beautiful and almost unrealistic views. The Moray Terraces are among the most beautiful Inca creations. Steve said that anyone who takes the time to explore the Cuzco-Sacred Valley area should take time to visit them.

Reading from a prospectus, Ping read that the Salineras de Maras, or Inca saltpans, have been used for centuries. They are allotted to the citizens of Maras. Each one gets a certain number of the plots, from which they keep the profits of the salt. Families pass the plots down from generation to generation like heirlooms.

The site was stunning. It was fifty-eight kilometers from Cusco in an isolated part of the valley. It consisted of thousands of mismatched white squares plotted along a steep green to brown hillside. It came out of nowhere, really.

Arriving in Ollantaytambo, they could see that it was a town and an Inca archaeological site in southern Peru, some sixty kilometers northwest of the city of Cusco.

Ollantaytambo was a passing point on the route of the Sacred Valley of the Incas up to a few years ago. Steve and Ping were pleased to see that Ollantaytambo was a modern city with all the services that visitor needed.

The city was dominated by a massive Inca fortress above the quaint village. Ollantaytambo was the best surviving example of Inca city planning, with narrow cobblestone streets that have been continuously inhabited since the thirteenth century.

Originally, this rural village was divided into blocks called canchas, and each cancha had just one entrance, which led into a courtyard.

Steve and Ping found a restaurant, since it was noon. The Kusicoyllor Restaurant seemed to be one of the tourist restaurants, offering quality in each one of their specialties, like pottages of the Novo-Andean cooking.

After ordering, Steve and Ping observed the people of the restaurant—if one of the missing squad was in Ollantaytambo, he would certainly be distinguished from the local personnel. There were many tourists, and the room echoed with the clamorous noise of everyone talking at once—and the more the noise, the louder the voices.

However, this was a tourist restaurant and it was expected that everyone would be discussing what they had just seen or what they would see next.

Suddenly, Steve's ears, highly trained to hearing French being spoken, got bits and pieces of a conversation. He could not quite understand what they were saying, but he was sure that they were saying it in French. They were six persons sitting at the same table, which was on the way to the restrooms.

Steve asked Ping to visit the rest rooms and walk slowly past the table so she could confirm that they were French tourists. She made no acknowledgement that she could understand French; she just passed the table going and coming. She confirmed that they were French.

Steve and Ping ate their meal, which pleased Ping much more than Steve. They discussed how they could go about making the rounds of the city's stores and restaurants looking for one or more of the escapees.

As they talked, Ping saw a man come out of the kitchen. He was not dressed like an employee and he went straight to the table where the French couples were talking. Steve had just enough time to turn around to have a look and see the man sitting at the table with them.

He had obviously joined their conversation. The man was in his late fifties or early sixties, so he could possibly be one of the escapees.

Steve had to find a way to open a conversation with the man. He could tell in a minute if he was French, and even distinguish between all of the different accents around the French national territory to narrow it down even further.

Steve wanted this opportunity, because he could just walk past and act surprised that French tourists were there, so far from home. This would open a conversation with them and he could then participate in their conversation.

Surprised to find an American who spoke French as well as they did, they all invited him to sit with them. Steve accepted, but said that he would only do so for a minute because his wife was on the other side of the room alone.

They all told him to have Ping join them, which Steve did immediately. Ping thanked them for their hospitality in French, as she had started to learn to speak some simple standard phrases.

The conversation then turned to where each person came from, which was a normal subject of conversation for strangers of the same country is meeting abroad.

When it came to the man from the restaurant, whose name was Xavier; he only introduced himself using his first name. Steve knew the names of the escapees and this man had to be Xavier Baysinger.

Steve let the conversation run its course without enquiring Xavier further. As their meal came to its finish, Xavier offered them all a treat—some real French Moka espresso coffee.

Seeing they were all appreciative of his gesture, Xavier explained that the flavor of espresso coffee depended greatly on bean variety, roast level, fineness of grounds, and the level of stovetop heat used. Due to the higher pressures involved, the mixture of water and steam reached temperatures well above 100°C, causing a more efficient extraction of caffeine and flavors from the grounds, and resulting in a much stronger brew when compared to that obtained by drip brewing.

He explained that he had the same supplier as the Paris & Ile de France Tea Rooms and Cafés & Coffee Shops chain of cafés in France and that the taste was a round taste that appealed to northern French consumers—that of roasted coffee with a premier grand cru Arabica from Brazil. This was why everyone prized a cup of coffee in his establishment.

The tourists readied themselves to leave and thanked Xavier for his hospitality and their amazement to find a Frenchman so far from home. They all left, leaving Steve, Ping, and Xavier at the table. Steve spoke first.

— Xavier, you have made a fine life for yourself here. However, I want to ask you something. First, do not get alarmed by my question, Steve cautioned.

— In reality, you are Xavier Baysinger from Mulhouse, right. Steve asked. You are one of the eight escapees from the 2nd DB at Bad Reichenhall.

— There is no need to worry; everyone who joined the SS Charlemagne division was pardoned a long time ago, Steve added before Xavier could speak.

Xavier's face reddened, and Steve and Ping could see his blood pressure mounting. He looked like he did not know whether he should bolt from the table or start talking to defend himself.

— Yes, Steve, I am Xavier Baysinger from Mulhouse and you are right; I was in the SS Charlemagne Division back during the war. I did escape with five other men from the same squad in an airplane leaving Stechovice with Otto Skorzeny, he explained.

— We flew to a place in Spain called Peniscola on the highway along the shore to refuel. We spent the night there guarding the plane and the special cargo, and then we were off to Madrid, he continued.

— We were given civilian clothes and Spanish passports. We took turns guarding the plane with its special cargo. Then, after about a week, Otto Skorzeny had us unload the crates from the plane and we took them to another airplane of the Empresa de Transportes Aéreos Aerovias Brasil S/A, which was a Brazilian airline at that time, he explained.

— Then we were off to Brazil and a new life, Xavier concluded.

— What happened next? What happened to the special crates you were guarding? Steve asked.

— From that point on, I knew nothing about the whereabouts of the crates or their contents. I

109

was given one hundred thousand US dollars and they told me to merge into South American life and never try to contact anyone again. I do know that some Spanish/Brazilian company hired Heintz, Kaufmann, Köhler, Bischwiller, and Haguenau for a while, Xavier went on.

— I know for sure that Kaufmann died mysteriously at that time, just before I left for Peru. His death was my reason for leaving Brazil quickly; I had the feeling that someone was eliminating witnesses to the activities surrounding the special crates, he continued.

— Do you have any idea what Heintz, Köhler, Bischwiller, and Haguenau became? Steve asked.

— No, as far as I know, they remained in Brazil and have been there ever since, Xavier answered.

— Look, we do not want to bother you anymore. You have been nice enough to answer our questions frankly and we appreciate that, Steve said.

That ended the conversation with Xavier, who felt relieved as if he had made a confession to liberate his soul after so many years.

When Steve and Ping were back in their car on the way to Machu Picchu, they discussed what they had learned from Xavier.

— Do you think he was telling us the truth? Ping asked.

— It is possible that part of it was the truth. However, I am sure he knows more than what he is revealing to us. We know that the remaining part of the Stechovice treasure was brought here in the area somewhere, and most likely, by the four remaining escapees form the squad, Steve reasoned.

— Let us get on with our touring at Machu Picchu and then we can think out what to do next, Steve suggested.

As Steve drove, Ping read the tourist brochure aloud.

— Machu Picchu, meaning "Old Peaks" is a pre-Columbian fifteenth-century Inca site located 7,970 feet above sea level. It is situated on a mountain ridge above the Urubamba Valley in Peru, which is fifty miles northwest of Cusco and through which the Urubamba River flows.

— Most archaeologists believe that Machu Picchu was built as an estate for the Inca emperor Pachacuti (1438 to 1472). Often referred to as

"The Lost City of the Incas," it is perhaps the most familiar icon of the Inca World.

Driving up there was a perilous adventure in itself because there were more than a dozen switchbacks with a rising elevation of 1,480 feet, not to mention the tourist busses encountered on the small mountain road.

They successfully arrived at the parking lot and took off on foot to see one of the Seven Wonders of the World. There were two main sections of the ruins of Machu Picchu. There are called the Urban and Agricultural Sectors, and they are divided by a wall.

The Agricultural Sector was further subdivided into upper and lower sectors, while the Urban Sector was split into east and west sectors, separated by wide plazas.

The central buildings of Machu Picchu used the classical Inca architectural style of polished dry stone walls of regular shape. The Incas were masters of this technique, called ashlar, in which blocks of stone were cut to fit together tightly without mortar. Many junctions in the central city are so perfect that it is said that not even a blade of grass fits between the stones.

Some Inca buildings were constructed using mortar, but by Inca standards, this was quick, shoddy construction, and was not used to build important structures. Peru is a highly seismic land, and mortar-free construction was more earthquake resistant than using mortar. The stones of the dry stone walls built by the Incas can move slightly and resettle without the walls collapsing.

Inca walls had numerous design details that helped protect them against collapsing in an earthquake. Doors and windows were trapezoidal and tilted inward from bottom to top, corners usually were rounded, inside corners often inclined slightly into the rooms, and L-shaped blocks often were used to tie outside corners of the structure together. These walls did not rise straight from bottom to top but were offset slightly from row to row.

The Incas never used the wheel in any practical manner. Its use in toys demonstrates that they knew the principle, although it was not applied in their engineering. The lack of strong draft animals, as well as steep terrain and dense vegetation issues, may have rendered the wheel impractical.

How they moved and placed the enormous blocks of stones remains a mystery, although the general belief is that they used hundreds of men to push the stones up inclined planes. A few of the stones still have knobs on them that could have been used to lever them into position; it is believed that after the stones were placed, the Incas would have sanded the knobs away, but a few were overlooked.

The space was composed of 140 structures or features, including temples, sanctuaries, parks, and residences that included houses with thatched roofs. There were more than one hundred flights of stone steps—mostly completely carved from a single block of granite—and numerous water fountains.

These were interconnected by channels, and water drains perforated in the rock, which were designed for the original irrigation system. Evidence suggests that the irrigation system was used to carry water from a holy spring to each of the houses, in turn.

According to archaeologists, there were three main districts of Machu Picchu: the Sacred District, the Popular District to the south, and the District of the Priests and the Nobility.

Steve and Ping toured around the village seeing the main places for about three hours. Steve then suggested that they get back to the car because driving on the mountain at night was a bit hazardous. Besides, they still had to get back to Cuzco.

The drive back was uneventful but they were both happy they had the opportunity to visit this famous place known all over the world.

Back in their room in the Andean Wings Hotel, they cleaned up to go to a late dinner. They went out into the city to look for a restaurant and found the Wanchaq neighborhood. There they found many Chifa restaurants. Chifa was the Peruvian version of Chinese food.

However, they preferred to try the traditional Peruvian food, Lomo Saltado (beef tips with tomatoes, onions, and spices, over a bed of French fries and rice), Aji de Gallina (chicken in a very good yellow sauce with olives and hardboiled eggs), or Papa Rellena (stuffed potato with beef, olives, hardboiled egg, vegetables, and spices).

While they were eating, Steve struck up a conversation with their waiter. He asked if there were many foreigners living here in Cuzco or even the area, while explaining his surprise at finding a Frenchman in Ollantaytambo.

The waiter answered in the positive. He did not know the foreigners personally, however, they were well known in the area because they were different from Peruvian people. Steve narrowed his question to foreigners especially speaking French or German. The waiter told them that they were lucky because there were two foreign men in Boca Manu.

One spoke French and the other spoke German. They were guides and co-owners of a tourist company that led excursions into the tropical forest. If they were interested, these two men could take them to Paratoari.

The next morning, Steve called InkaNatura to reserve a one-week tour for two. They were to leave in two days so they had time to prepare. A trip into the rainforest was no small affair.

Two days later, Steve and Ping flew to Boca Manu with three other couples in the small aircraft. When they arrived, they split up and took a ninety-minute boat ride on the Rio de Madre de Dios to the lodge. The ride was great and the lodge was fantastic, with nice bungalows, no electricity, and beautiful grounds on the river. They soon learned that the food was also great at this lodge, and that was no small feat considering the logistical issues. All of the staff at the lodge was friendly and very professional.

The comfortable Manu Rainforest Lodge was situated close the banks of the Manu River. They were now deep in the pristine Manu rainforest in the Night Manu Rainforest Lodge

The tourists had all finally met up and the rest of the tour proceeded smoothly enough. Steve and Ping were stuck in the front of the boat (the last seats left), which meant that they couldn't hear anything said by the guides or anyone else, and were constantly sprayed with muddy river water...but were happy enough to entertain themselves.

The scenery was amazing...the Apurímac River was just a tributary of the Amazon river, but was at least one half of a mile wide in places, with trees two hundred feet high, right down to the water's edge.

It had rained constantly for the last two days, so the river was high, and there was the periodic crash of another tree falling into the river from the eroded banks.

The Apurímac River is the source of the world's largest river system, the Amazon River. It rises in Peru's southwestern cordilleras, seven miles from the village of Caylloma, and less than one hundred miles from the Pacific coast.

It flows generally northwest past Cuzco in narrow gorges of up to nineteen hundred feet; twice as deep as the Grand Canyon in the US, its course interrupted by falls and rapids. Of the six attempts so far to travel the Apurímac in its full length, only two have been successful.

After 454.04 miles, the Apurímac River joins the Mantaro River and becomes the Ene River at 1,325 feet above sea level; then after joining the Perené River at 984 feet above sea level, it becomes the Tambo River; when it joins the Urubamba at 859 feet above sea level, the river becomes the Ucayali, which is the main headstream of the Amazon.

The lodges Steve and Ping stayed at were all comfortable enough, once they got used to sleeping under a mozzie net with ten-centimeter-long cockroaches crawling along the top.

Steve and Ping of course had no problems finding a billion mosquitoes per square meter. Other than that, there were the usual jungle animals to deal with...monkeys, giant otters eating fish, turtles on logs, caimans, and birds, lots of birds.

Normally, this would not be a problem, but they seemed to have joined a tour full of ornithologists.

In the evenings, everyone met in the large dining room where they feasted on Peruvian specialties and international food for those who were not adventurous enough to try tasting something else for a change.

The guides circulated among the guests and ate at a different table each night. The first night they had the pleasure of a Peruvian guide at their table so they talked and talked about the rainforest and the rivers.

On the second night, they had the pleasure of a guide speaking with a French accent. He introduced himself as Louie Bockel. Now Steve and Ping were on full alert and asked question carefully.

— You are French right. Whatever brought you here to live in Peru? Steve asked, after a while.

— I was brought up in France but the war changed everything for me. My entire family was killed during the Second World War so I was fed up with living there.

— I just started trekking around South America until I wound up here and formed a company with a Peruvian friend, Louie explained.

— We live in Paris and I have been in France for over twenty-five years now. I am retired but I do journalistic work from time to time, Steve explained.

— My research on an item of the Second World War brought me to a story about a squad of men from the SS Charlemagne Division who escaped in 1945. Louie, I have been looking for these men. The French government pardoned them and they have nothing to fear from the law...French or international, Steve continued.

— I think that you are one of these men and if so, you could only be Heintz, Kaufmann, Köhler, Bischwiller, or Haguenau, because I have already met and talked to the others—Xavier Baysinger, Georges Ribbonet, and Kurt Dammerskirch, Steve suggested.

— OK Steve, I am one of the escapees. My real name is Louie Haguenau, not Louie Bockel.

At that point, Steve told Louie everything that he knew about the escapees and especially the part concerning Otto Skorzeny and the flight from

119

Stechovice to Spain with the special crates that finally wound up in Argentina. Steve also told Louie that he knew the treasure was hidden somewhere near the magic circle.

Just as Steve mentioned the magic circle, Louie's eye opened wide and he began to redden. Steve could see a few beads of sweat rolling slowly down the side of his face.

This man knows a lot about the treasure, I am sure, thought Steve.

— Do you know where the others are, have you seen them lately? Steve asked.

— Louie, what do you know about the treasure that was in the special crates brought to Argentina? Steve questioned further.

Louie sat there with a pensive look on his face. He was either thinking about "WHAT" he should say or "IF" he should say anything to this American stranger. At any rate, Louie felt attacked on a subject that he feared.

— Steve, first I can tell you that Köhler is no longer with us. He was attacked by a panther and so badly mauled that he died before we could fly him out back to a hospital. His grave is the other side of the camp, Louie explained.

—   I think the best thing is that we talk about all this with Piers Kaufmann, who is my partner here. This camp and the tourist company are ours, Louie explained.

—   Piers is with a group and he will not be back before tomorrow evening, Louie concluded.

—   Do not be late or miss the safety briefing tomorrow morning, right here in the restaurant, cautioned Louie. It is very important, he warned.

The camp was so isolated that there were no telephone lines or any other means of communication, so that evening, Steve was deprived of his sacred Internet and Ping was overjoyed.

Ping was an astute observer of people and things that occur; she told Steve that after Louie left them, she saw him on a satellite phone calling someone. His demeanor was such that she could tell that he was certainly talking to his partner Piers. They seemed to be arguing about something.

Steve and Ping attended the safety briefing the next day and it was interesting that all of the warnings were given to the unknowing tourist who would dangle his hand in the river as they advanced and would pull back only a hand of bones. The ferocious fish found in the river in this area would eat all of the flesh.

The tourist guides had to be on constant look out for the tourists to keep them from getting hurt because of the very beautiful but extremely dangerous environment in which they were living and traveling. The briefing was very professional, demonstrating things to beware of with a slide show.

After the briefing and lunch, the day seemed to drag on waiting for Piers to arrive with his group of awe-struck tourists. They were all very tired and happy to be back at the base camp.

They were all chattering about what they had seen and how wonderful it was. They all seemed to agree that this part of the world must be taken care of to preserve all that they had just witnessed.

After Piers had seen to his group and tethered the boat they had used, he cleaned up after the excursion. From afar, Steve and Ping could see him working, but they did not want to disturb him.

They preferred that he come to them, as they had requested. When Piers was finished, he struck out and headed for the office where Louie was working on the camp's paperwork.

Steve and Ping did not approach the office but they could hear shouting. Apparently, they were arguing, and most likely about the contact with Steve and Ping.

Everyone went to the evening meal and it was something to see. The ambient sound level was at least the same as a power mower, 107 dB, whereas it should normally be around 60 or 70 dB.

It was the excitement of all the people in the group returning today that kept the ebullition of their experience going as long as it could. Steve could only wonder what they had seen and done today to cause such a reaction.

Steve and Ping sat at a table as far as they could from the group, but even so, it was hard to carry on a conversation. They had flown up with two other couples sitting at their table. They seemed to be in an ecstatic state in anticipation of what they would see and do in the coming week.

If Steve and Ping had any idea of what was in store for them, they would not be so pleased to see all of these people rejoicing.

As the meal wore on, the excited tourists started to leave, carrying on outside and in their sleeping quarters. Finally, there was some peace and quiet in the dining room.

Louie and Piers came in and grabbed a bit to eat. They sat at a table across the room and gave frequent glances at Steve and Ping as they talked.

Moments later, both Louie and Piers came over to their table and sat down. They had waited until the dining room was almost empty. Louie introduced Piers to Steve and Ping and said that they were going to talk about what they knew.

— Mr. and Mrs. Santa, we do not appreciate you digging into our past. We know that the French government has pardoned our past but that period in time is long behind us and we do not appreciate opening up a part of our lives that is most sensitive, Piers said.

— Let me tell you what I know and then you may ask any question you want to OK? Piers asked.

— You know that Köhler is no longer with us. He died from a panther before we could get him to help, Piers explained.

— As for Heintz and Bischwiller, they were here a long time ago, but it has been years since we have seen or heard from them, Piers went on, trying to close doors before Steve and Ping could open them.

— Louie tells me that you are interested in the Stechovice treasure, Piers said, startling Steve, who did not think they would talk about it so readily.

— Yes, we are interested in finding the remainder of the treasure because we have already found the first half in France in the Yonne, near Cravant, Steve said.

— What can you tell us about it? We are not here to involve you in any way; we just want to find what we can about the treasure. We now know what has happened to most of the missing Charlemagne squad that escaped, except for the whereabouts and what happened to Heintz and Bischwiller, Steve concluded.

— We will talk about the treasure, but not here in the camp. I prefer to take you both on a trip to see the Pyramids of Paratoari; we will talk about it then. You two and I will take a boat at seven tomorrow morning. Nothing will be lost because you will see the Pyramids, Piers ordered.

— How long will the trip take Piers? Ping asked.

— We will just be gone for the day. We will be back before sundown tomorrow evening, Piers explained.

With that, their meeting broke up, as they had to see to the guests' comfort before turning in for the night. Steve and Ping returned to their sleeping quarters and talked about the plan for the next day. Ping was very suspicious and Steve knew that she had the knack of being able to judge persons and situations very clearly.

Before turning in, they both prepared small things that might be useful if something went wrong. Neither of them trusted Louie and Piers. However, it was also possible that they would just go out, learn about the treasure, and come back with no incident.

— Ping, I want us to both be on our guard tomorrow. Closely observe what Piers does while we are with him, Steve cautioned.

— Do not worry darling, I am as worried as you are, and I will be glad when we are safely back here in the main camp, Ping said.

— Anyway, I love you so much that I will not let anything happen to you again like in Austria, Ping said, as she took Steve's head in her hands and looked deeply into his eyes, kissing him so that there was no doubt about her care and her deep love for him.

— Let's get a good night's sleep, said Steve, without knowing how much this last sleep would be critical to their survival.

The next morning they were up at dawn, ready to meet Piers and get on with it. Piers did not keep them waiting long. He went straight to the boat docks with a picnic bag and prepared it for the trip as Steve and Ping walked over.

— Get in and let's get going. We have some traveling to do in the boat today, ordered Piers.

Steve and Ping each carried a small knapsack that they stored away at the front of the boat. It was a fifteen-foot Saturn SD740 inflatable boat with a passenger capacity of eight persons. It had twin 40-hp Mariner outboard motors. There were four 6-gallon portable fuel tanks at the back of the boat.

They were off in a flash, the wash from the passage of the boat licking the shorelines until they arrived in the larger part of the river. They road for about three hours at high speed; then Piers suddenly slowed the motors and aimed for the shore. Steve could see a small landing place indicating that someone had been there many times before.

Piers told them to get out and help pull the boat as far on shore as they could and then he tied a rope from the boat to the closest large tree to secure it.

— We will go on foot from here, said Piers, as he grabbed the picnic bag and canteen of fresh water.

Steve and Ping had brought just small plastic bottles of water they had taken from the dining room last night.

Off they went on a trail that had been walked on often enough to keep the vegetation away. They walked for another hour or so and suddenly came to gigantic pyramids situated at the foot of a mountain, the Sierra Baja of Pantiacolla (Pantiaj Colla in

Quechua language means "the place where the princess gets lost").

The set was four kilometers long, and there were approximately twenty-two pyramids, of which some were six hundred feet. There were other large semicircular or rectangular formations in the same perimeter. The whole setting made Steve think of an immense sanctuary, even a whole city, gobbled up in the jungle.

— Here may be the remains of an ancient Inca city. Maybe even the vestiges of Paititi, the queen of the South American lost cities, said Piers.

— Come over here and we will eat and talk, Piers ordered by indicating a large block of stone they could all sit on.

Piers spread a cloth and placed sandwiches in plastic wrappers out for each of them, with an apple as desert. Hungry after the long walk, they all ate heartily. When they had finished and cleaned up the plastic and paper, and stored it back in the picnic bag, Piers said that they could ask him about the treasure.

— First, you should know that we originally brought it to Argentina where Juan Perón's government protected us and allowed us to settle in the southern regions of the country, Piers said.

— However, Peron's act was not gratuitous. We were obliged to leave parts of the treasure with him and his wife Eva. She met secretly with Nazis who were part of the entourage of Otto Skorzeny, Piers said.

— For instance, we were obliged to give her the Amber Room decorations that had been stolen. She became even richer after obliging us to give over some of the paintings we had brought in the crates, Piers said, with certain disgust in his voice.

— We did get about $6 billion in jewels and gold. There were especially bags full of diamonds. What Peron left split into a few parts for funding of the Fourth Reich. They brought the remainder here for safekeeping, not only from the world but also from the Perons and the bandits you can often find in these countries.

— No one could ever find it here unless they knew where they were looking. Certain members of Odessa today know of its whereabouts, but only a select group even knew of its existence. How you ever discovered so much about it is a wonder to me, Piers concluded.

— So in fact, we are sitting next to a certain remainder of the Stechovice treasure right here...where we are now, Steve said.

— You must know that when Heintz and Bischwiller left, they took a sizable part of the treasure with them. However, the remainder of the treasure is under one of these pyramids, Piers replied.

— I am curious as to why you are letting us in on the secret so easily, Ping said.

— My dear Mrs. Santa, it is only because you will never see it or leave here, Piers said as he drew a pistol from his vest.

— Why do you want to hurt us, we can do you no harm, Steve suggested, desperately trying to think a way out of this new calamity.

— Steve, that is simple. Odessa lives today. It has just modernized and is infiltrating all positions of influence in Germany and France. One day, we will come back into power and, of course, we will need the funding that the Stechovice treasure represents for us, said Piers, sounding like some Nazi propaganda person.

As he was talking, Piers was gathering some vines from the ground and stones. The vines were everywhere. It was part of the rainforest reclaiming its territory.

130

— These vines are like leather, you will never be able to undo them, said Piers as he handed a few to Ping while keeping them covered.

— Tie your husband up tightly with these and be careful...I will check them after I have tied you up too, he commanded.

Ping could do nothing but obey.

She turned the vines around and around Steve's wrists, with his hands behind his back. She did not try to do anything stupid because Piers was in full control of the situation.

When Ping had finished, Piers ordered her to step away from Steve so he could check the tightness of the vines.

He sat Steve down on the block where they ate lunch and then went to Ping, who was standing about ten feet away.

He told her to turn around and put her arms behind her so he could tie her up in the same way as Steve. She did so, but she was alert, and in a mind frame of attack.

As Piers approached her from behind, and when she felt him touch her arm for the first time, she attacked. She dropped lower on one leg while using the other leg in a sweeping motion, which knocked Piers off his feet. Unhappily, he managed to keep the

131

pistol in his hand, and to Ping's surprise, while lying on the ground; he did a rotation movement with his legs causing Ping to fall as well.

He caught Ping off guard and Piers was back on his feet before she could regain an attack position. His hand with the pistol handle came down on Ping's right shoulder with such a force that it dislocated her shoulder.

Ping gave a piercing cry because of the excruciating pain she felt. Her right arm was useless. She cried out when he moved her arms behind her back to tie them solidly.

Piers then searched their pockets for anything that would help them to get out of the vines securely binding their wrists. The vines were so tight that they were drawing a little blood as the captives tried to move.

— Now you have us; what are you going to do with us? Steve asked.

— I am going to let you take a pleasure ride in a boat, Piers answered.

With that said, he ordered them to start walking, but strangely enough, it was in the opposite direction from the river on which they came there.

I wonder just where he is taking us, Steve thought.

Steve could see that Ping was in pain while walking.

If he was going to kill us, he would have already done it, Steve thought.

They walked slowly along a trail for what seemed like a mile of two. Then they came to a slope that was rather steep. Piers told them to go down the slope.

— You are going to untie at least one arm so we can grab onto the trees as we go down; otherwise, we will fall and roll to the bottom, Steve said.

— Besides I want to fix Ping's shoulder, he concluded with a firm and determined voice.

— OK, but no monkey business or you will get shot right here and now, replied Piers, as he moved behind Steve to undo the vines binding his hands behind his back.

Steve went over to Ping and undid her vines. He touched her shoulder to see what had happened.

Steve made sure that Ping's upper arm was in its resting position, perpendicular to the ground. Then Steve had Ping lie down. He helped her gently get down, knowing that the relocation would more bearable if she was lying down.

Steve placed her elbow at a 90° angle and rotated her arm and shoulder inward, toward her chest, to make an "L" shape. Slowly but steadily, he rotated Ping's arm and shoulder outward, being sure to keep her upper arm stationary.

He told Ping to make a fist on the injured arm, and then he held on to this wrist with the other arm and pushed slowly. When her lower arm was just past 90° to her chest, Steve could coax the shoulder back into the shoulder joint.

— Please try to bear the pain. I know it will be painful but you will be relieved right away after I get your shoulder in place, Steve said encouragingly.

Steve had to repeat the same process until the shoulder relocated itself, on the third try. Ping could hear the popping sound when her shoulder popped back into its joint. Ping felt relieved immediately.

— Thank you, Steve darling. I feel better now. At least I am not in constant pain like before, but my shoulder is weak and I do not want that to happen again. Where did you learn to do that? Ping asked.

— I took first aid training that covered a wide range of help for an injured person, Steve said.

— Come on you two. Steve, tie her up and then get back here so I can tie you up again, Piers commanded.

Steve moved her arms behind her gently and then tied one of them firmly. He then got up and let Piers tie up one of his arms firmly to his belt behind his back.

They all started down the hill, which was very hard to negotiate using only one arm to cling to each tree and bush as they went down the long slope. When they reached bottom, they were on another well-trodden trail. Piers had Steve tie both of Ping's wrists behind her and then Piers tied up Steve. This time Steve used the old trick of joining his fingers together to be able to keep his wrists a little bit separated. This would give a small bit of slack once Steve stopped pushing his wrists apart. It would give them a chance to get them undone later.

Piers ordered them to walk along the trail for about a half an hour, until they came to a large river. There seemed to be a river on each side of the mountain where the pyramids were built. Steve had no idea of its name and only an idea of where they were.

They arrived at a small landing on the river, where they saw two reed boats. Each boat was flat in the water, with a slightly beveled edge. The bow looked like a horse's head. The stern just dwindled down to the level of the water.

Vines similar to those they were tied up with held the reeds making up the boat together. The rest of the boat was flat and there were no seats. One could see that its intended purpose was fishing.

One could only suppose that the indigenous people here had been using this kind of boat for thousands of years.

— All right, get into this boat, both of you and sit down, commanded Piers.

— Here Ping, let me help you. I will get in first and you can use me as a brace to keep your balance until you can sit down, instructed Steve.

As they stepped into the reed boat, Steve saw a long pole supposedly to control the boat's movements and push it away from rocks.

Steve had kept the pressure on his wrists so hard that a little blood showed under the vines. This is what he wanted Piers to see that they were firmly attached.

Piers summarily inspected their attached wrists and then got out of the reed boat and pushed it out into the large river.

— Adieu, my friends! Have a great journey in the reed boat, but watch out for the rapids, Piers said, laughing aloud.

136

— If the rapids do not get you, the crocodiles deep in the Amazon rainforest will, said Piers, waving to them as if he was saying goodbye to friends out on an excursion.

As the reed boat moved out more and more to the center of the river Steve could see that there was a swift current there. It was time that he got his hands free to be able to steer the boat as much as he could with the long pole.

Steve released the pressure he was exerting on his wrists and he could feel that the vines were a bit looser than before. Steve inched his body over closer to Ping so that they were back-to-back. This way Ping was able to touch the vines on his wrists.

Without saying a word, Ping understood the purpose of the maneuver Steve had just made and she scraped away at the vines in Steve's wrists. The further the reed boat moved to the center, the rougher the ride was becoming. Water was splashing over the low edges of the reed boat getting them wet.

Then Steve remembered that Piers had said the vines were like leather. He remembered that if you soaked leather in water it stretched out longer, however, if you then allowed it to dry, it became tighter than before. Therefore, he had a risky decision to make.

— Ping, scoot toward the back of the boat where you can sit on my legs as I bend backward into the water. I just want to get the vines soaked for a minute then I will sit up again and we can move back to where we were and try to get the vines off of me, since they should be looser, Steve shouted, as the roar of the fast moving river was gaining speed and volume.

They squirmed toward the back of the boat and Steve sat in an upright position right on the edge of the boat until Ping got to him and rolled over his legs. The only thing Steve was worried about was Ping's weight.

Would it be enough to allow me to sit up again once I have soaked my wrists in the river? Steve was thinking.

Anyway, there was no other solution and they had to try this way to get free. Once free, they could try to maneuver the reed boat to the shore and avoid getting into the rapids they could hear in the distance.

Steve let himself lay down backward so his hands touched the water. It was like doing a sit-up, but with your hands tied behind your back, which did not help anything.

Steve stayed in this position for about a minute. Then he told Ping to brace herself and put as much of her weight as she could onto his legs. Steve then did a kind of lateral rolling movement instead of sitting up straight.

This kept the counter-balance weight of Ping at its minimum usage. Steve finished his rollover to bring himself out of the river and wound up lying parallel to Ping.

He could not avoid taking advantage of the situation of being face to face. Steve moved his head closer and kissed Ping tenderly, then passionately.

— Wow, Steve Santa, you cannot control yourself when you have a woman in this position in front of you, can you, Ping said with a deliciously tempting smile on her face, in spite of their situation.

They turned around and sat back-to-back again. Steve pulled his wrists as close as he could, and felt Ping moving the vines. Effectively, the little slack Steve had forced when Piers tied him up became much slacker since he had gotten the vines wet. They slipped over his hands, still a lot of effort, but easier than if they were not wet.

It took what seemed like hours to get the vines off one hand so that it was free. Thinking that it might be harder to get the hand that Piers tied first free, Steve scouted around to see Ping's back. With his free hand, he loosened the knots on the vines binding her hands together.

In a moment she was free and rubbing her wrists to ease the pain. Then she untied Steve's other hand so that there were now free.

Now we have to get out of this death trap before something happens, thought Steve.

Steve told Ping to keep the vines they were now free of and use them to make a sort of lasso around the head fixture on the boat. Then she could use that to be more stable in the boat when they were in rough water.

They heard the roar of the rapids coming closer and closer. Steve knew that this would not be a piece of cake to get through in one piece. However, since they could not get the reed boat closer to the shore they would have to ride it out. Unfortunately, the reed boat seemed to have a mind of it's own.

As they entered into the rapids, Steve could not help himself from thinking of the poem *The Charge of the Light Brigade*, by Alfred, Lord Tennyson:

Half a league, half a league,

Half a league onward,

All in the valley of Death

Rode the six hundred.

"Forward, the Light Brigade!

Charge for the guns!" he said:

Into the valley of Death

Rode the six hundred.

They entered into the rapids with Ping and Steve clinging to the vines around the head figure at the bow of the reed boat. It was just like rafting on the Colorado River in the states. Terrible forces came into play and the reed boats with its two occupants were thrown around as if they were leaves.

The roar was deafening. They tried to shout with their heads almost together, but it was extremely hard to understand what the other was saying. Water was splashing all over the little reed boat.

The rapids gave way to a narrower river moving very fast between the walls of a canyon that reminded Steve of the Grand Canyon. The canyon walls were

141

hundreds of feet high, so there was no way they could get out, even if they could steer the boat to a shoreline, so they continued their rollercoaster ride down the river.

— Keep hanging on with all your might, Steve said, as he moved his body onto Ping's body to keep her from moving when the reed boat hit a rock or if they had to go into other rapids.

— I am dear. This is so frightening that I will never go to another amusement park as long as I live, screamed Ping in return.

The river moved them along at a high rate of speed for what seemed like an hour or two. Then Steve and Ping could hear the roaring sound louder than before.

They soon found out that they were starting into another set of rapids, which had many boulders that could turn the reed boat over if it hit one the wrong way, and spill them into the cold river, taking away any chance for survival.

They somehow got through these rapids unscathed, still clinging to the vines attached to the head figure of the reed boat. They came out into another canyon, but with smaller walls.

They were still too high to climb to safety and, anyway, they could not find a landing place or even get close to the shore.

142

This time they came to a junction of two rivers. The river they just came down seemed to join into a larger river with an even stronger current. They were thrown this way, then that way at the junction.

I wonder how long Ping's and even my strength will hold out in this kind of turbulence, Steve was thinking, just as the new and larger river seemed to get calmer.

They floated in the center of the new river for a long time, clinging to each other and trying to keep warm by keeping their bodies close together. The cold was numbing them. It seemed like hours had passed since they had been on this reed boat, and the light was starting to fail.

The sun was setting quickly now and they would be left without sight in this tormenting river ballade.

Judging by the descent factor of the river starting from a height of about eight thousand feet, which was that of Machu Picchu, the speed of the river would be faster than most, which are about seven miles an hour. Steve figured that it must be about double, or more like fifteen miles an hour.

They had been on the reed boat for eight hours now; therefore, he calculated they had traveled nearly 120 miles already. Seeing as how the rivers flow toward the Amazon River, they must be close to Bolivia now, and right smack in the middle of the rainforest.

This was not a good sign for them. It was now night and it was pitch black. All they could do was listen carefully for the warning that they might be coming to another rapids or even a waterfall. Since Ping was shivering a lot, Steve rubbed her body, arms, and legs to keep her blood flowing.

Steve also felt the numbness gaining on his body, but they had to resist. The night seemed to be eternal, but then Steve saw the first rays of light coming from the east; now, he at least knew that they were traveling eastward. This seemed logical since he knew that eventually they would wind up in the Amazon River, if they ever got that far.

They continued going downstream for hours on end. The river seemed to be endless and there was absolutely no sign of life, modern or indigenous, anywhere to be seen.

Steve knew that they had to get water soon or they would become dehydrated. The sun was high in the sky. A thick lining of rainforest trees and dense vegetation grew along the river banks.

Both of them saw the sandy bank of the river ahead, so Steve grabbed the pole and started pushing the reed boar toward the bank.

They knew that they had to get water and some sort of life sustaining substance if they were to survive. The first thing they thought of getting were the water

144

lilies—the largest flower in the world, which grows up to six feet long. They took several onto the reed boat to collect water when it rained.

The next thing they saw was bromeliad. The most common bromeliad specie was Steve's favorite tropical fruit, the pineapple. Bromeliad plants come in a variety of colors like purple, blue, orange, and red. They were growing all over the rainforest on rocks, in the soil, and few even grow on other Amazon rainforest plants and tree trunks.

These plants were life-sustaining plants, as their leaves overlap each other and store rainwater. They collected a few and some vines to fasten them onto the reed boat.

Then Ping saw a cashew tree, which produces yellow, orange, or red fruit commonly known as the cashew apple. Ping knew about the cashew apple even if it was unknown in the US. The cashew apple can be eaten or squeezed to make juice. Ping knew that the cashew apple contained many antioxidants, including vitamin C.

Then they found some white trillium flowers, which had three petals, three sepals, and three leaves. Ping told Steve that if they chewed on to white trillium leaves, it would help cure snakebite. It also helped curing fevers, she told him. They harvested a water lily leaf full and attached it to the reed boat with the rest of their food stock.

145

Steve found a small tree that he bent in all directions until it came out of the ground. Then, using a tree that had fallen over another tree on the ground, he used this as a leverage point and broke off the roots. He pulled the smaller branches off one by one to make a staff to be used for protection and guiding the reed boat.

— Thank God, you took a survival course, Ping. I never had the opportunity to do so. Now I believe it would really be helpful, Steve proclaimed.

— It was a very hard survival-training course, and we were on our own with no food or water to cross a part of jungle near Jinghong in the Yunnan province of China. I am very thankful that I took it, Ping said.

They were now seemingly equipped to confront the rugged nature of this river going straight through the rainforest. Now they had a chance to make it somewhere. There must be somebody civilized out there that could help them get back to civilization.

They could not have known, but each night they passed by the woodcutters campsites. These men were deforesting the rainforest.

With their reserves full on the reed boat, they took time to dry out and try to estimate where they could be. However, of course, they had no maps and only a summary knowledge of the area.

They tried to think out their situation. *Would it not be better to try to cross the rainforest until we came to someone who could help us?* This was too risky and, anyway, they now had a reserve of life sustaining foods and water, so there was nothing preventing them from trying to go down stream.

There was less risk in the water than in the rainforest with all the snakes, animals and spiders you could think of.

They pushed off from the sandy bank and Steve pushed the reed boat more into the center of the river to keep away from any crocodiles that could be lurking near them.

— Ping, I will always try to steer the boat, but from now on you must not only protect yourself by hanging onto the vines we collected and attached to the head like a safety belt, but you must, at all costs, keep the food and water as safe as you can. If it is lost while we are going through rapids, do not bother trying to get it back because that would be too dangerous, Steve instructed.

— Yes dear Steve, I will, but I also want you to be very careful too because you only have the one thick vine attaching you to the reed boat. If

147

something happens to you and I cannot get you back onto the boat then all is lost, Ping exclaimed.

They continued their journey on the river for two more days and nights. According to Steve's estimation, they were about one hundred miles inside of Brazil. They had crossed Bolivia at its northeast tip. They were now getting closer to the real Amazon River.

On the afternoon of the fifth day, there was a terrible rainstorm. Steve and Ping could not see even ten feet ahead of their reed boat. The noise of the rain was extremely loud and drowned out any other noise.

Before either of them could sense the danger, they were on top of it. It was a waterfall of what seemed to be a great height. They were going over the edge just when they realized what was happening. Steve had just enough time to dive on top of Ping to protect her from whatever may happen at the bottom of the falls.

Over they went, lock stock and barrel. When they hit the bottom of the falls, the reed boat did cushion their fall on the rocks somewhat; but it also threw them apart, off the boat, and into the cold frothing water. They were sucked underwater and struggled to regain the surface.

They were at the end of their strength and both Steve and Ping were starting to blackout.

Was this how we are going to end, just when we were better prepared to make it, thought both Steve and Ping.

As everything was getting black, Steve felt a hand on his arm. He thought Ping might have pulled him upward. Steve blacked out completely. He was in a sort of dreamland, but it was sure that he was unconscious.

Steve had terrible nightmares about anything and everything until he heard Ping's soft voice in the distance somewhere. *Are we both dead and gone to meet our savior?* Steve could not feel anything, but he heard Ping calling his name incessantly and anxiously.

As Steve emerged from the lethargic state he had been in for two days, his first sight was his beloved Ping on her knees, bending over him. He was lying on some blankets placed on the ground in some sort of hut.

— Oh my God, there you are Steve. I was so worried. I thought that this time I had really lost you. You were under the water so long that I was sure you had drowned, Ping said. She kept talking so much and so fast that Steve could not even get a word in edgewise.

When Steve saw the opening, an Amazonian Indian walked in. He spoke Spanish and only a few words of

149

English, so they tried to communicate as best they could.

Steve tried to make him understand that they were Americans, but he did not seem to understand fully because Ping was so different from anyone he had ever seen before.

He had seen the white men cutting down the trees and clearing out the forest, destroying their home, but he wondered what this woman could be.

Steve pulled Ping down to him and kissed her very tenderly so that nothing could be mistaken that she was his wife.

The man tried to explain with words, drawings, and hands and feet, that he and his friends from their village had seen them go over the falls and immediately went to save them.

The turbulence was so great, but they got Ping out quickly. They had to work hard to find Steve because he was pinned underneath a rock by the strength of the underwater current.

After a day or so Steve was feeling his oats and started exploring the surrounding areas of the encampment they were living in.

His host was the head of the village. His name was Aikana. Aikana was one of the few that could manage a few words in English he had learned from the white rubber plantation men.

Aikana was proud of his tribe and their live in the rainforest. He wanted to explain all this to Steve and Ping because they were being persecuted. The white rubber men and white outlaw lumbermen were destroying their land.

— We live in huts made of babacu straw, with a small entrance. We make hammocks of cotton and tucum palm, use bows and arrows for hunting; paint ourselves with genipapo and urucum, also using an arara feather in our earlobes and lower lip.

— We make pots and chicha (a fermented drink, made from maize), and caicuma (made from manioc), which are drunk during rituals. Until we were contacted by the white men, we lived from hunting, fishing, and collecting, planting small gardens of manioc, maize, etc."

— In earlier times, we used to pierce our ears and lower lips, but the older ones said they had never used ear ornaments, or other adornments on their lips.

— Agriculture is slash-and-burn. Each plot is about two hectares in size, an area big enough to maintain a small family for a year.

— More than one family from the village, usually in-laws, can also work the plots.

— Generally cultivated near the villages, the plots are worked in a consortium system with different types and varieties of crops. Those most cultivated are manioc, both domesticated and wild, maize, yams, potatoes, banana, rice, peanuts, pineapple and watermelon.

— The most important plant is manioc, planted specifically to make flour, the main ingredient of our daily diet.

— Hunting is an eminently male activity and is normally carried out at night in previously reconnoitered places, under the canopy of a fruit tree where the hunter installs his "hide," a specially prepared place to await the approach of the animal.

— Another method used is to paddle slowly and attentively along the river at night, using a torch to light up the banks of the river, searching for any animal that comes to drink water, bathe, or feed. Another hunting method we use less frequently is to go into the forest during the day to look for animals.

— The weapon we most use is the rifle. Bows and arrows are almost never used. Sometimes we use traps or dogs. The animals most hunted are the wild boar, paca, tapir, deer, armadillo, and monkey. The birds most hunted are the mutum and the jacu. We eat Cayman meat.

— We fish a lot because there is an abundance of fish, a situation maintained by the absence of overfishing, because the river rises and runs through the interior of the Cinta Larga Indigenous area before entering Arara territory.

— Fishing is an almost every day activity that involves men and women of all ages. Children in small canoes navigating from one bank to another in search of the best place to fish are a common sight.

— Brazil nuts are one of the most accessible sources of food protein in our daily diet, present in almost all homes. Besides our family consumption, we sell the nuts in the local market.

— In recent years, the Arara have managed to trade large quantities of nuts in regional and national markets, with the support of outside agencies, making them an important source of income for the families.

— I know that you are not going to like this, but insects are also part of the Arara menu. The most popular of the edible insects are the larva that lives inside the trunks of palm trees called coró de coco.

— We can find them because of the noise they make inside the trunk, and we eat them fried, with or without oil. The children especially love them, Aikana concluded.

Steve and Ping could see that they were not only a proud people but also self-sufficient in this rainforest area, where a civilized person would certainly starve.

Steve and Ping could understand that Aikana was making a propaganda pitch for their benefit because they were really at war for the survival of their way of life that they loved so much.

Steve made a promise to himself that when they returned to Paris he would research information on the Arara people. He would find out that the Arara Indians in the Brazilian Amazonia were fighting for their survival against waves of armed loggers, ranchers, and colonists who are destroying their forest homeland.

The situation was so volatile that the Arara dare not hunt further than ten kilometers from their village. Traditional hunting trips, where men go off for days in search of game, are impossible, as the Indians would not risk sleeping in the forest at night.

Imprisoned within their own land, one Arara described leading "a life of terror," as the forest echoed with the constant roar of chainsaws felling mahogany and other valuable hardwoods.

Government officials had reportedly surveyed the Arara territory (called Cachoeira Seca) with the aim of reducing its size and handing out tracts of the land to loggers and settlers. It had not yet been demarcated (physically mapped out with markers) by the government.

The Banat logging company bulldozed a road through the territory and now land grabbers and loggers were opening up feeder roads and penetrating deeper into Arara land.

The Arara once inhabited a large area, but due to disease and violent conflict with outsiders, they now numbered only two hundred people.

The Arara's recent history has been one of persecution and violent contact with jaguar skin hunters, rubber tappers, settlers, and, lately, loggers.

For years, they eluded contact and fought to defend their land. FUNAI, the government's Indian affairs department, tried desperately to make contact with the tribe before the Trans Amazonia Highway cut through the heart of their territory.

Steve and Ping had fully recovered from their ordeal. They told Aikana that they thanked him for their help and very generous hospitality. However, it was now time for them to leave and go back to their civilization.

However, Steve told Aikana that he was a part-time journalist and that he promised to write some articles in his journal to draw attention to the situation of the Arara people in the hope that it would help to put an end to the persecution they were undergoing.

—   Aikana, how can we get back to civilization from here? Steve asked.

—   My friend, we will take you to a point near the logging men where we will leave you. We cannot approach them because they will try to shoot us with their rifles, Aikana explained.

—   I warn you, these men are ruthless and dangerous people. Be extremely careful when you are around them, Aikana concluded.

—   We will leave tomorrow morning when the sunrises, Aikana said.

They had a good night's sleep on the blanket-covered ground. It seems that you can adjust to just about anything when you are obliged to.

The next morning, Steve and Ping said goodbye to all the friends they had made and then they left with Aikana leading the way.

They made their way through the rain forest for about three hours until Aikana signaled them to stop and crouch down. They had approached a clearing where there were trucks and men. It seemed like two of the men were fist fighting. The others were cheering on their own friend in the fight.

It was a noisy spectacle and a disgusting display of raw violence for nothing, but probably an insignificant incident involving who would drive today or some similar stupid excuse to fight.

Aikana indicated to Steve and Ping to enter the clearing from a point that was at 90° from where they had originally approached the clearing, to hide the real direction from which they came.

Steve clasped Aikana's hand in a warm display of thanks and comradeship while Ping kissed him on one cheek to show her thanks for all they had done.

As Aikana slipped back into the rainforest, Steve and Ping entered into the clearing shouting a loud hello.

That was enough to bring the fistfight to a startling halt. The group of men just stood there in wonder and amazement at the sight they beheld.

Then there was a lot of discussion about seeing a woman way out there. They clearly indicated they wanted to take advantage of her. The lumbermen approached them.

Apparently, they were lacking any respect for anything. If they killed Indians just for sport, why not take advantage of this frail woman and have their pleasure with her.

When they were close enough, two sturdy men grabbed Steve by the arms. It was useless to struggle because they were extremely strong men.

One bare-chested man, who had been fighting and who had gotten the better of his opponent until Steve and Ping appeared, came too close to Ping. He was about to grab her when her Wing Chun auto defense mechanisms sprang into action. The man was on the ground with a broken arm faster than you could count one-two-three!

This seemed to frighten and encourage the others and another man tried his luck, but a quick kick in the groin sent him to his knees crying like a baby.

Still encouraged and not having learned their lesson, two men tried to approach Ping at the same time. Ping flipped one backwards to the ground with a broken wrist while Ping held the other with a thumb pressure point on the back of his hand, making it impossible for him to move because he was in so much pain.

Ping shouted to them!

— Have you had enough to leave us alone now?

158

— No honey, let us see if you will give us what we want if we do not harm your boyfriend, one of the men holding Steve said.

That straw broke the camel's back. Ping swung into action like a tigress defending her cubs.

Of the eleven men, three were already on the ground and useless to fight so Ping attacked two on her way to where two men held.

The first two went down in a flash with damage to certain nerve points, making it impossible for them to get up again. By the time the two men has realized what Ping had done, she was upon them.

Her first action broke the arm of the man who had not spoken. Then she turned her attention to the man who had spoken and who still had Steve's arm in his hands.

— Careful, your life is at stake. Let him go or you will suffer the consequences, said Ping.

The man started hurting Steve by bending his arm so far behind his back that it could break or come out of joint.

That was enough to see. Ping was somehow in the air, coming at his neck with one of her feet. The man dropped Steve's arm and fell to the ground with a heavy thud.

— Anyone else wants to try his luck, said Ping, with a vicious air about her, showing that she was serious.

— I have not killed up to now but if you continue, I will not be able to control my automatic reactions and some of you will be dead in a few minutes, Ping warned.

The others backed away and some helped the wounded men to sit or stand. One of them came forward to talk with Steve and Ping.

— What do you want? the man asked.

— Well, now that you have some wounded men, I suggest that you had better take them to the nearest village or city where there is a dispensary or hospital to get help for them, Ping said.

— At the same time, you will take my husband and me with you, she continued.

— Put the wounded into the back of the truck, and you...you will drive us. We will sit in the cab with you. If you think of trying anything else, beware that the Wing Chun works just as well in close quarters.

They rode the bumpy dirt road all the way to Porto Velho without any incident. They went directly to the little hospital. As the injured men started entering into the hospital, they all threw looks at this little Chinese woman who had gotten the better of them, as if they were children.

It was as hard to believe as it was for them to accept that this seemingly weak little woman beat them.

They went to the center of the city of Porto Velho. From there they took a taxi to the Ji-Paraná Airport, about eighty miles away. Brasília, the capital of Brazil, was an eight hundred mile flight, and they had to get the US embassy's approval to fund the tickets as refugees.

The first consul of the US embassy met them. He had checked the veracity of their story with the US embassy where they were registered, and the US embassy in Paris, where Steve and Ping were well known.

The first consul's name was Jeff and he took charge of everything. He had reserved a hotel for them and he arranged for the US embassy in Peru to get and forward their baggage they left in the Andean Wings Hotel in Cuzco, as well as return the 4Runner Trail to the Hertz office.

—   Mr. and Mrs. Santa, get a good night's rest, then come to the embassy and ask for me. We have to get you new passports, Jeff said.

161

— Hey Jeff, thank you so much for all this help. Tomorrow, I will explain what happened to us. Right now we need a good shower and bedtime to recover from everything, Steve said, as they took the key and headed for their hotel room.

Once in their room, Steve and Ping clung to each other. They kissed and gave each other tender caresses, staying like that for a while and savoring their lives together.

Both had a good hot shower to wash off all the rainforest dirt and a part of the adventures they had just lived through, then they were off to bed. Steve and Ping kissed each other good night and were both asleep before their eyelids closed.

The next morning, they both woke up at nine o'clock, but stayed in bed to enjoy just being in the comfort of the hotel bed, looking at each other and talking about what had happened, as if talking about it would smooth the harsh emotions they had just endured.

The finally got up, and had breakfast sent up while they were showering and dressing. With breakfast finished, they were off to the US embassy in a taxi.

When they arrived at the US embassy, the Marine on guard was suspicious at Ping being an American citizen, so Steve told him to call Jeff to come to get them.

Jeff brought them to his office. He offered tea or coffee, and both Ping and Steve accepted. Jeff took them to get passport photos inside of the embassy. Normally the embassy would not do this, but since this was an urgent case, they made an exception.

After the photos, they went back to Jeff's office, where Steve and Ping related all that had happened to them and why. Searching for the missing SS Charlemagne squad and the Stechovice treasure was quite an adventure. It was dangerous because someone forced them to go down the river in the rainforest.

Jeff spoke to them about the Arara people and their fight to regain control of their territory. It was a well-known subject, but it was a very unpopular subject in view of the economic issues involved.

By the time they discussed their adventures and the plight of the Arara people, their new passports were ready. Jeff handed them to Steve and asked what their plans were.

We have to get back to France; our research on the missing squad is not finished. We have the last two men to find, and probably the remainder of the treasure.

— Jeff, please keep our adventures out of the news. If they do not know we are still alive, we have an advantage over them, Steve requested.

163

— Anything you say, Steve. Look, it has been a real pleasure to meet you, Steve and Ping…and if you come back to Brazil, look me up. I always have a good martini and lots of conversation waiting, Jeff offered, as they left his office.

Back at the hotel, Steve arranged the flight back to Paris. Just at that moment, the bellhop knocked at the door with their luggage from the hotel in Cuzco Peru.

They were ready to leave on the flight tomorrow at 7:00 p.m., departing Brasilia and arriving in Paris Orly at 6:20 p.m.

Back to Paris

After arriving in Paris, a run through the passport section, and a quick run for baggage, they were on the taxi stand, waiting for the next cab for Paris.

Within three quarters of an hour, they were back in the security of their Montparnasse apartment.

— Wow, Ping...it sure is good to be home again. I think I will start appreciating the apartment more and more, Steve said.

— You can believe that, my dear husband, and in the future, we are really going to have to limit out adventures to more civilized and moderate adventures. Don't you think so too, darling? Ping said, as she cuddled up to him on the couch in their favorite place.

— Yes, I agree to some extent, Ping, but you can never know where a story will lead you...and by the same measure, what you will have to go through.

— However, you are right; we need more time together. We must find time for just the two of us with no one trying to harm us. Just our own little cocoon, Steve said, as he started cuddling closer and took Pings foot for a long and delicious foot massage.

They took a few days off and did nothing but visit Paris and walk around the romantic places hand in hand, cuddling together as they walk. They went to a few of their favorite restaurants and even tried some new ones at Ping's suggestion.

After about the third day, Steve became restless, he had to get back into the search for the last two members of the missing SS Charlemagne squad.

Steve knew that they would have come from Brazil and that Odessa had certainly provided them with forged papers and background. They were probably posing as Brazilian or Peruvian business men or industrialists.

However, where could they be in France? Piers and Louie were sure that Heintz and Bischwiller had returned to France with lots of money to integrate themselves into the modern Odessa movement in Europe. Steve looked for their first names, because these could be an indicator as to their current identity.

Looking up the military records, Steve found that their old full names were Conrad Heintz and Kurt Bischwiller. Taking the problem from there, he made a study of Brazilian or Peruvian men immigrating to France and who built an empire in finance or industry.

It was very hard to discern post-war immigration from South America to France. It could be any one of two dozen men, and Steve had to be very careful not to disturb the innocent ones while not alerting the wrong ones.

He felt like he was doing a tight rope act; there were dangers if he fell on either side. He was sure that the real Conrad Heintz and Kurt Bischwiller were ruthless Nazis with an insane mentality who would stop at nothing to avoid revealing their secret.

Killing was not a proposition; it was the standard operating procedure.

Ping was preparing for a new conference that was the continuation of a previous one concerning Nuclear Cold Fusion, held in the south of France at the Cadarache Centre in the community of Sainte-Paul-les-Durance in the Province-Alps-Cote d'Azur.

Steve was a bit jealous because Ping would stay on the Rivera for two weeks, a great place to be at any time of the year. It was only thirty miles from Marseilles, fifty-five miles to St. Tropez, and seventy miles from Cannes.

Oh well, she merits it and I cannot have everything, Steve thought.

Steve got back to Googling people and companies to see who was on the board of directors. Who was their president, the largest shareholder, and so on? He had gathered a host of information, but he would need some clarification from someone at the Paris Brazilian embassy to understand what he had found.

The Brazilian embassy was a dead end because it only registered Brazilian persons entering into France. Once they were here, the suspected persons could have done anything, and easily contacted the modern day Odessa movement to get fake authentic French credentials.

Steve knew there was another source of information that would certainly be one of the best. This person had hunted down Nazis right from the end of the war and had important files of information on many of them.

He was a lawyer called Serge Imfeld. Serge and his wife were activists known for engaging in Holocaust documentation and anti-Nazi activism. They were involved in finding many Nazi personalities and bringing them to prosecution for their war crimes. President Mitterrand awarded France's Legion of Honor serve.

Getting an appointment with Serge Imfeld was no small affair. However, Steve was determined; he obtained a half-hour interview with Serge Imfeld himself in the presence of his wife.

When Steve went to the appointment, he was ushered into a large office with books and files all over each piece of furniture in the room. Serge got up and came to welcome his guest.

— Mr. Santa, I understand you are an American and we seem to be doing the same kind of work, he said, after introducing his wife.

— Yes, Mr. Imfeld, I have been on a special investigation of an event concerning the 33rd Waffen SS Charlemagne Division, Steve said.

— I do not know if you are aware of the events with the 2DB in Bad Reichenhall in May of 1945, and especially concerning the French General Leclerc, Steve continued.

— Not many people know that a squad of eight men escaped execution. They escaped and left for Czechoslovakia, where the German 7th Army controlled the sector, Steve went on.

— For an American, you are extremely well informed, and if my information is correct, you are the American who helped discover part of the Stechovice treasure in Cravant, France, not too long ago, Serge intervened.

— Yes, Sir; I have my sources here in France. I have been living here for more than twenty-five years and I have a lot of friends and contacts.

Steve then related all that had happened while trying to find the missing squad, but he did not talk about his source, the colonel in Sacy who got him onto the story. This was too personal and the colonel has specifically asked Steve not to reveal his identity to anyone.

— Mr. Santa, what is the problem that brings you to me today? Serge asked.

— Please call me Steve. I have found six of the men of this squad and I am about to reveal to the authorities the whereabouts of a good part of the treasure that has not yet been found. However, I am still missing two of the men and I have traced them back to France.

— They have been aided by the modern day Odessa group to get new authentic identities and they are here living among us. I want to expose them, even if they received a pardoned for their participation in the SS Charlemagne division by the French government.

— For me they are still guilty of reselling part of the Stechovice treasure that was part of the SS war loot. I believe that there is no prescription for this crime, so I want to return the treasure to its rightful owners and bring them to justice for harboring this treasure looted during the war, concluded Steve.

— Mr. Santa...Steve, I perfectly understand you and your motivation and I will provide you with any help or information that it is in my power to give you in this matter, Serge said.

— We know that the modern day Odessa group is still active and we have been bombed to prove it. I will open my files to you but I am sorry to say that my personnel are working on a very important Nazi personality we want to bring to justice so they will have very little time for you except to point you in the right direction in our files.

— Therefore, I want you to remember that the reading and analysis of these files is your responsibility, Serge explained.

— Serge, I cannot tell you how much I appreciate your cooperation in this matter, and I am a part-time journalist, so I know how to sift through information by myself.

— I would not think of subtracting from your own efforts, which are much more important than mine are, Steve agreed.

— Steve, when it concerns the Nazis, there is no little or big affair. To us they are all important; we are just approaching the end of this affair and must see it through with a maximum effort is all.

—   Otherwise, we all would be glad to participate
in your search with you, Serge Imfeld
concluded.

Serge's wife then took Steve to an adjacent room
where two men were pouring over loads of
information. Serge introduced Steve to the men and
requested that they point Steve in the right direction
for his research.

They gave Steve the information concerning the
richest men in France and other European countries.
It was his job to sift through this immense pile of data
to try to find the needle in the haystack.

Incidentally, while Steve was analyzing the
information, he suddenly realized that Serge's
organization had infiltrated a part of the modern day
Odessa organization and lots of the information he
found here was very current.

Steve was able to extract several suspicious name
files with current photos—that seemed to be
clandestine photos.

However, the men were completely identifiable and
many were industrialists who were in the news
anyway.

One that caught Steve's attention was an Alsatian
wine grower and negotiator living in Alsace for only a
few years.

His name was Heintz Eberstark. Eberstark is not a rare family name. If you can find a village name for the birth, death, or marriage of your most recent Alsatian relative, you have a very good chance of finding many more of them.

In France, every time you move, get married, have children, die, and so on, you have to go and register with the Mairie (city hall), so they would have good records of the major events in people's lives.

Steve had a gut feeling, an intuition about this man. Therefore, he started to look up the family name in the Alsace city records. He started with Mulhouse, the city where the escapees came from.

In searching back in time, he found that there was an Eberstark family and that in the generation preceding that of Conrad Heintz, the daughter of the Eberstark family married the only son of the Heintz family named Ryker Heintz.

Steve then searched the Mulhouse city hall records and found that a son was born to this couple in 1923 making him twenty-one at the time of the second war, and his name was Conrad.

That was enough for Steve. He was sure that he had found his man. Everything pointed to confirm that the Alsatian wine grower and negotiator in Heiligenstein was indeed the missing SS Charlemagne squad member Conrad Heintz.

Since Steve knew about Alsatian wines and was a lover of Gewürztraminer, he decided to make a trip to Heiligenstein to meet this man and find a way to confront him with his past.

Steve arranged a TGV train trip to Strasbourg with a rented car waiting, and again he reserved a room in the Mont Sainte Odile Convent for a few days.

Upon arriving in Strasbourg, Steve picked up his car and headed to the convent. The familiar faces of the nuns working there greeted him. They recognized him from his last visit, which was not so long ago. They all asked where his beautiful and talented wife was. Steve explained that she was obliged to remain in Paris to prepare for a conference.

Steve had already reserved a rendezvous with this Mr. Heintz Eberstark for an interview concerning an article he was to publish in an American Wine Magazine published monthly called *Food & Wine*. It was a very good publicity base and an article in that magazine would enhance sales by at least 25 percent, or so Steve explained to obtain the meeting.

Mr. Heintz Eberstark was anxious to receive and inform this American journalist on his products. He offered a selection from Gewürztraminer to the sparkling Vin Fou of the Jura.

Steve arrived at the appointed time in. Heiligenstein. The city of Klevener is located at the foot of Mont Sainte Odile. Heiligenstein is famous for its "Klevener" single cepage in Alsace. Its wine vocation dates back to the third century in Roman times.

The distant origins of the village remain a mystery. It is perched at an altitude of 250 meters between vineyard and forest still. It acquired its current name in 1460. Heiligenstein is only fifty miles from Mulhouse.

Since he was going to confront Mr. Heintz Eberstark, Steve took the precaution of having Gendarmes stationed just down the road, ready to act on a moment's notice.

Steve was ushered into an immense office with beautifully finished mahogany furniture and several racks of wine on demonstration for visiting customers to see.

The opulence of the office indicated that this man was immensely rich. Steve took it in stride without letting on that he was impressed.

After the standard introductions, they started talking wine.

— You will dine with me I presume. It is the hour, and I would like you to sample some of our Alsatian delights in addition to our wines, said Mr. Heintz Eberstark.

— Please call me Heintz, Steve. You will see some of our best traditional dishes today he boasted.

Steve of course accepted and they sat at a dining table to the side of the immense office room where they could see the vines on the hillside. During the meal, Heintz launched into the sales pitch he had developed over the years.

— Gewürztraminer is the most typical Alsatian wine. Gewürz means "spicy" in German. It is the main characteristic of Gewürztraminer. Traminer means "coming from Tramin". The grapes come from a small city in south Tyrol of Austria. Gewürztraminer is the name of a grape, but also the name of the wine made from the grape!

— You know that Gewürztraminer was originally grown in Alsace around the nineteenth century. The grapes now cover roughly 20 percent of the vineyards in the region. It is obviously in Alsace where Gewürztraminer grapes give the best results.

— The wine is delicious, fruity, and with strong aromas—a very perfumed and flowery bouquet. Gewürztraminer is sweeter than a dry wine like Riesling, Heintz went on.

— You can see that this thick and rich wine, which can age, is better with sauerkraut, sausages, and the Alsatian cheese Munster, curry seasoned dishes, Chinese and Mexican cooking, and other spiced dishes. Gewürztraminer is also served as a dessert wine, he suggested.

— Gewürztraminer reaches its finest expression in Alsace, where it is the second most planted grape variety and the one most characteristic of the region. It grows better in the south of the region. Styles range from the very dry Trimbach house style to the very sweet.

— The variety's high natural sugar means that it is popular for making dessert wine, both Vendange Tardif and the noble rot-affected selection of noble grains.

— Gewürztraminer replaced a grape called Klevener or Savagnin back in the old days. Nowadays Klevener wines are grown only in the village of Heiligenstein and surrounding villages.

— Klevener is a dry white wine with slight spicy flavor, and while less aromatic than Gewürz, it should be drunk young. It is one of my very best specialties and I can make you a very good deal on it.

— Steve, around Heiligenstein the grape known as Klevener de Heiligenstein, is probably Red

Traminer (Savagnin Rose) rather than a true Gewürz, the Heiligenstein wines are more selective than other Alsace Gewürztraminers.

— This is a specialty, that your readers would like to know about since it is unknown in France, he concluded.

The meal had drawn to its end and it was a succulent meal with just the right combinations of wines and tastes. Steve had enjoyed it so he let his host know his appreciation of the efforts he had made.

— Now Heintz, or should I say: Conrad Heintz? I want to talk with you on another subject, Steve said to the startled man.

— First off, I want to tell you that I am not interested in your participation in the 33rd SS Charlemagne division. I know you were an escapee with your squad of seven others.

— I have already met with Kaufmann, Köhler, Haguenau, and Baysinger all from Mulhouse, and Dammerskirch. I have not yet located Mr. Bischwiller, but I will soon meet him face to face, as I am with you, explained Steve.

— I know that you are all pardoned by the French government for your participation in the SS Charlemagne division so that is not what I am here to talk to you about today,

Steve continued, as Heintz sat in his chair, turning red and sweating profusely.

— I always knew that one day my past would catch up to me and here we are, Mr. Santa, he said in a feeble voice lacking the confidence and self-control he had when Steve first walked into the office.

— Explain yourself Steve. What are you after from me? Heinz asked.

— Conrad, you are a part owner of a treasure of Nazi war loot smuggled out of Europe from Stechovice Czechoslovakia at the end of the war, Steve explained.

— This is the reason I am here today. I have been looking for you and the others for months and you are the second to last on my list. I want to have you make restitution of your part of the war loot the Nazis smuggled out to Argentina, of which you took your share and came back here to lead a normal life that is a lie.

— You must face justice for your crimes Conrad, concluded Steve.

Just then, Steve pushed the "send text" button for the message he had prepared to get the gendarmes into the office as quickly as possible to avoid any blood shedding.

It worked smoothly; the gendarmes were rushing into the office in a matter of two minutes. Conrad surrendered himself to the arriving gendarmes.

Steve reminded the Gendarmes that Conrad was to be incommunicado until the interview by Steve, the gendarmes, and the special judicial unit for investigating this type of crime. Then the state would bring charges against people accused of genocide, war crimes, or crimes against humanity in France or abroad.

Kurt Bischwiller and Odessa

Steve and Ping already knew that Kurt Bischwiller would be the hardest to find since he had re-integrated into normal society by the modern day Odessa organization.

Steve's ideas naturally turned toward the extreme right wing parity in France "Le Front National" because that is where the neo-Nazi power was currently wielded and a person like Kurt Bischwiller could become integrated easily with no questioning of his background.

"Le Front National" was a popular political name already used in France when the foundation of the National Front is to put in the context the events that followed the crisis of February 6, 1934.

The French won a list of reforms undertaken by the Popular Front—working time from forty-eight to forty hours per week with no pay cut and employees receive twelve days of paid leave (the period of paid leave increased to three weeks in 1956 in 1969. Then four and finally five in 1981), wages were increased from 7 to 15 percent of the collective agreements already in place.

The February 6, 1934 crisis refers to an anti-parliamentary street demonstration in Paris organized by far-right leagues that culminated in a riot on the

Place de la Concorde, near the seat of the French National Assembly.

It was one of the major political crises during the Third Republic (1871–1940), and it entered the popular consciousness, especially that of the socialists, as an attempt to organize a fascist coup d'état.

The National Front had, however, a virtual existence until 1938. It was replaced by Le Front National (FN) a French far right, Nationalist political party, founded in 1972 by Jean-Marie Le Pen.

However, it was not a very peaceful organization internally. There were constant divergences between Supporters of Le Pen and of the "national-conservative" and a tendency to oppose "nationalist revolutionaries" closer to the vice-president and Third Position ideologies.

The split between the vice-president and Le Pen started on July 16, 1997, during an FN meeting near Strasbourg. The general secretary of the FN, initiated the hostilities against the vice-president by criticizing "ideological racialism" theories supported by FN members close to the Nouvelle Droite and former members of the Club de l'Horloge.

He also advocated a return to more "paternalist" approaches of immigration issues, in the French colonialist tradition. However, the most extravagant statements made by the highest personalities of the Front National clearly demonstrated its neo-Nazi character.

The organization was beleaguered by legal problems and Holocaust denial condemnations.

On January 7, 2005, Jean-Marie Le Pen declared in the far-right newspaper *Rivarol* that the Germans' occupation of France "hadn't been so inhumane." On September 13, 1987, he had already referred to the Nazi gas chambers as "a point of detail of the Second World War." In accordance with the 1990 Gayssot Act prohibiting Holocaust denial and other forms of negation type statements, he was at the time sentenced to pay 1.2 million Francs (183,200 Euros).

Bruno Gollnisch, MEP was the leader of the European parliamentary group Identity, Tradition, and Sovereignty since its creation in early January 2007. The same month He was sentenced to three months of prison on probation and 55,000 Euros in damages and interest by Lyon's tribunal correctional for the "offense of verbal contestation of the existence of crimes against humanity." On October 11, 2004, Gollnisch declared:

> "I do not question the existence of concentration camps but historians could discuss the number of deaths. As to the existence of gas chambers, it is up to historians to make up their minds."

Ultimately, Gollnisch was not found guilty by the French judicial system.

To further illustrate the neo-Nazi character of this organization, many FN activists were prosecuted for illegal acts. On May 1, 1995, four FN activists pushed Brahim Bouraam into the Seine River.

In December 1997, skinhead David Beaune was pronounced guilty in Le Havre for the death of Imad Bouhoud.

In 1998, Ibrahim Ali, a seventeen-year-old Frenchman with Comorian origins, was shot dead by three FN billstickers, members of the FN's militia, the Department of Protection-Security (DPS).

The whole organization perfectly resembled the old structure of the Nazi Party from the 1930s.

Steve gave a lot of thought as to how to discover the real identity of Kurt Bischwiller, especially since he would be involved in one way or another in Le Front National. He would be involved either within its structure or externally through financial aid provided to finance the political party. Le Front National almost won the French presidency in 2002 by winning 17 percent of the vote compared to the 19 percent of Jacques Chirac in the first round of elections.

To accomplish this feat, Le Pen needed enormous amounts of financing, supplied by serious sympathizers to his cause and those who were Odessa members or associates.

Odessa was not the type of organization you joined and quit at-will. Once you are in, you are hooked for life

Steve began the monumental task of listing and categorizing each of the personalities likely to be Kurt Bischwiller.

To build such a database, Steve requested information from his journalist friends, who were more than happy to oblige. Steve's database was growing by the day and thanks to the power of the Internet and computers, the project would have required tens of hands classifying information.

The analysis of this database reduced the number of men who could possibly be Kurt Bischwiller to twenty five.

Steve used the hypothesis that Kurt Bischwiller would be associated with the Front National. Cross-referencing these twenty-five men with those associated in any way whatsoever with Le Front National further; he reduced the number to five men.

With this reduction accomplished, the only way to go further in the detection of Kurt Bischwiller was to be in physical contact with each of them for a further evaluation.

It was not at all easy to introduce yourself into a politico-social sphere, regardless of its tendencies. The case of the Front National with its fascist activities and almost certain links with the modern day Odessa organization made it extremely difficult to make yourself accepted.

Steve and Ping were analyzing the situation and methods of approaching these five men.

— I do not think you can bring yourself into contact with these men through a political approach. You have never been extreme right, and even if you are able to approach them, they will certainly make a background check on you, Ping suggested.

— You are right, Ping. We have to find a neutral approach, like their favorite sport or social activity, like art, music, or anything that could be a common basis for mutual interest and acceptance, Steve proposed.

— Money Steve! Money is their common denominator outside of their association with the Front National, Ping declared.

— You have got it Ping! Money is something that brings people together even more so than politics. The only problem with that is I am not a millionaire like these five men. I am financially free from any worries, but I am not in their class, Steve concluded.

That evening, when they were dining and discussing the problem, they reviewed all of the possible means of entering into the intimacy of these five men. This was looking like a very long project, because it would not be a good idea to approach them all at the same time.

— Steve, there is something major we have not touched on yet. How are you going to identify the right man once you have been accepted by each one? Ping asked.

— I have my little idea on that subject Ping. However, I need to confirm my idea on the Internet before I can say for sure that it would work, Steve said.

— My idea is that all of the SS soldiers had their blood type tattooed on their arm. This was a procedure to aid in blood transfusions in battle conditions, Steve concluded.

— The idea sounds good Steve, but they are not stupid enough to leave the tattoo on their arm. Odessa must have thought up the solution to that problem long ago, Ping exclaimed.

— Of course, they would have disguised it, cut it off or some solution like that, but it would leave a scar or some trace indicating that something was there at some point in time, Steve continued.

— Let me check all this out on the Internet first, Steve concluded.

After the meal, Steve and Ping went for a walk down in the Latin Quarter where there were many people roaming around. They sat at a café, had a tea, and watched the people go by. This was one of many Parisienne favorite pastimes. They always enjoyed the Latin Quarter because the ambience was always joyful and filled with strangely dressed people.

The Latin Quarter of Paris is the "petit city" that rarely sleeps. There are many bistros, cafes, brasseries, boulangeries, jazz clubs, boutiques, bookshops, and tourist shops, and you can hear voices of the multi-lingual personalities and "tourism" at its height. The street food sold among the street performers is the best for food to eat while roaming with the crowds.

The next morning while Ping went out to meet a prospective customer at the Chinese embassy, Steve clicked away on the Internet.

Steve found information on Wikipedia confirming that the SS blood-type tattoo was mandatory, in theory, to all Waffen-SS members, except members of the British Free Corps. It was a small black ink tattoo located on the underside of the left arm, usually near the armpit.

It generally measured around 7 mm (0.28 inches) long, and was tattooed roughly 20 cm (8 inches) above the elbow. The tattoo consisted of the soldier's blood type letter, A, B, AB, or O.

The Rhesus factor discovered in 1937, was not understood during World War II, so it was not considered. In the early part of the war, tattooing was in Gothic-style lettering, while later on they were printed in Latin style.

The purpose of the tattoo was to identify a soldier's blood type in case am unconscious solder needed a blood transfusion while his Erkennungsmarke (dog tag) or Soldbuch (pay book) were missing.

Generally, the tattoo was made by the unit's Sanitäter (medic) in basic training, but could have been applied by anyone assigned to do it at any time during his term of service.

Before the tattoo was developed, a wounded soldier needing a transfusion was matched with another with the same blood group. If there were no reaction within ten minutes of the blood transfused between the patient and donor, it would be assumed the blood group was the same.

Not all Waffen-SS men had the tattoo, particularly those who had transferred from other branches of the military to the Waffen-SS, or those who transferred from the Allgemeine SS, the "general" or non-military SS. Some non-SS men also had the tattoo. If a member of a branch of the Wehrmacht was treated in an SS hospital, they would often have the tattoo applied.

Although the tattoo was widely used in the early war years, over the course of the war, gradually it was applied to fewer and fewer soldiers, and toward the end of the war, having the tattoo was more the exception rather than the rule.

The application of the tattoo to foreign volunteers was apparently an issue of contention, with some, such as the British Free Corps not required to have it, while other foreign units did not object.

Very little specific information exists regarding the tattoo and foreign units, but it is claimed by some that the men of the (French) 33 Waffen-Grenadier-Division der SS Charlemagne had the tattoo applied.

Steve immediately thought of calling Georges Ribbonet, one of the escapees who they had met already.

A quick phone call to Mr. Ribbonet confirmed that the 33 Waffen-Grenadier-Division der SS Charlemagne had the tattoo applied and he was sure that all of the eight escapees had the tattoo.

With this confirmed without a doubt, there was still the problem of finding a way to enter into the sphere of these men.

One other problem remained...how to see the left armpit of each man. This was not going to be easy, Steve thought to himself.

Ping returned from her appointment at the Chinese embassy and was very happy to have signed on for four interpreting sessions for an important Chinese Director. The sessions were held in Paris, London, Bonn, and Rome. She was thrilled to be part of these negotiations and to travel around Europe.

—   Ping, if I can get away from this project, I will come and meet you in Rome. I have only been there once and I did not have much time to see anything, Steve suggested.

—   That is a good idea, Steve. Besides, Rome is the last stop so we can take some time together and do some touring, Ping answered.

—   Have you figured out how you are going to check out the five men yet? Ping asked.

—   It all comes down to two problems, Ping. The first is how to get into their social sphere and the second is how I can get to see their left armpit, Steve said laughing at the thought of looking at men's armpits.

— Steve, I certainly cannot and will not help you on the second problem, but I have an idea for the first problem, Ping stated.

— What is your idea Ping? Steve asked.

— That is the easy part Steve. These men are in high financial spheres and would certainly be known to or even associated with our dear friend Gonzague de Sarlat, Ping suggested.

— You are an angel my dear Ping. I knew that there was a reason I married you, Steve said laughing aloud. He loved to tease Ping about anything and everything.

— I will get on to Gonzague. It has been a long time since we have seen him, Steve concluded.

Steve and Ping had met Gonzague de Sarlat while they were searching for the secret of the last Parfait. He was a noble and very rich industrialist and landowner around Sarlat. Gonzague de Sarlat is one of the most eminent French Cathar personalities in France. He was a very influential person in industrial and political matters.

After the affair of finding the Cathar treasure, Gonzague had become a close friend, enough that he would lend his private jet to Steve and Ping on a rare occasion. The confidence between them was total.

Steve called Gonzague on his normal business line asking his secretary to have Gonzague call him when he had a free moment. Steve had Gonzague's private cell phone number, but he did not want to use it unless it was an emergency or if Gonzague was travelling and could not be reached at the office or home.

Within the hour, the phone rang; it was Gonzague on the line.

— Steve, how are you and Ping? It has been too long since we saw each other. We have to find some time to be together. What brings you and why didn't you call on my private cell phone? Gonzague scolded.

— Gonzague, I know you are a busy man and I avoid disturbing you unless there is something important. I need to come to Sarlat to see you and explain a project I am working on. I will need your help, but you must hear out my project. I will not talk about it on the telephone so we must meet in person. When would you have time to meet me in Sarlat? Steve asked.

— My friend, you know that you are welcome in my home any time, so why don't you just come to the house in Sarlat and we will spend dinner together and talk about your project. Will both of you come, I would love to see your ravishing Ping again? Gonzague asked.

— No, Ping is preparing an interpreting session and I will only spend the night. I must return to Paris the next day. You will understand when you have heard my explanation of the project, Steve answered.

— So be it, Steve. I will expect you tomorrow at the house. I will leave instructions and prepare an Internet connection for you. Just come to the house when you arrive. There will be someone to greet you and set you up.

They hung up and Steve immediately got on the Internet.

Sarlat-la-Caneda was about 350 miles south of Paris in the Dordogne department in Aquitaine in southwestern France.

There is no quick or direct way to get from Paris to Sarlat, so Steve reserved the TGV to Bordeaux, which took three hours, then connected to a train to Sarlat, which took another two hours. Steve could easily see why Gonzague had his own private jet to get him directly in and out of Sarlat-la-Caneda.

The next day, Steve was off early to get the TGV at the Gare Montparnasse, which was only a stone's throw away from his apartment. The ride down to Bordeaux was pleasant and he found himself in Sarlat rather quickly. Steve took a taxi from the train station to Gonzague's residence.

His chateau was in the heart of the Black Perigord, a magnificent castle with a majestic view over a hill. It was about nine hundred square meters of living space, ten bedrooms, six bathrooms, beautiful reception rooms, a swimming pool, a caretaker's house, and outbuildings, everything within a park of about twenty hectares.

Gonzague had built a small aerodrome two miles from his chateau where his private jet could land; he shared it with all of the other aircraft owners in the area.

Steve adored coming to this area of France because the area was known for its cuisine, more particularly its products related to ducks and geese, such as foie gras. It was one of the truffle areas of France, historically the most famous. Périgourdine wines included the famed Bergerac (red and white) and Monbazillac. He knew that Gonzague had an excellent chef and they would have a feast that night.

Arriving at the Chateau, Steve was greeted by Benedict, the person who arranged everything in all matters for Gonzague. Gonzague familiarly called him his "Nuncio".

Benedict brought Steve to his room and asked if there was anything else, he could do. Steve thanked him and said that he would take a walk in the park in a little while. Steve asked what time Gonzague would arrive. Benedict gave a vague answer, which could only mean before dinner.

While he walked in the park, Steve felt the serenity that reined there. It was the perfect place to relax after the stress of working, especially for Gonzague, who had a real empire to manage.

Steve walked for an hour and was sitting on a bench overlooking the hill when Gonzague came to meet him. They were both happy to see each other because they had built a bond between them during the search for the Cathar treasure.

— How are you my boy; you are looking good, exclaimed Gonzague.

— Well to tell you the truth Gonzague, I have recovered completely from problems I have experienced with the project I want to talk to you about, Steve explained.

— Hey, let us go get some of Louie's Périgourdine cooking and we will talk about it, commanded Gonzague.

Steve, Benedict, and Gonzague all had an aperitif, and then they went to the great dining room. Benedict participated in all discussions and Gonzague had perfect confidence in him because he also made some decisions in Gonzague's absence.

The entrée was a Périgourdine salad with Foie Gras and smoked duck slices on a bed of greens with cherry tomatoes. The main dish was Beef Wellington with a Périgourdine Sauce; they drank an excellent red Bergerac wine. The conversation remained general until the end of the meal. When the coffee was served, Gonzague asked Steve to tell him about his project.

Steve explained the incidents that occurred in May 1945 in Bad Reichenhall concerning the German 33rd Waffen SS Charlemagne Division composed of Frenchmen who joined the German Army. Gonzague had heard rumors about the incident. He was surprised to learn of the escape of the eight men of the squad and all that Steve and Ping had done to find them and the remaining part of the Stechovice treasure.

— Now I understand why you said you were recovering. A gunshot wound is nothing to play with. I see that you are still in the business of adventure, Steve Santa, Gonzague exclaimed.

— I have found all of the escapees except one, who has certainly returned to France now, aided by the modern day Odessa organization, Steve explained.

— I have narrowed the list of persons likely to be the last escapee, but I need help to get into their social sphere in order to detect which of them is the last escapee, continued Steve

— My problem is in order to approach these men close enough and be intimate enough to check their armpit to see if there was a marking, I cannot just walk up and say here I am. I need an introduction, Gonzague. I am a journalist and acceptable in their social sphere, but I must be invited, concluded Steve.

— My dear friend, I perfectly understand what you are trying to accomplish and why you are doing it. Now let me say this. If I am to engage my person by introducing you into these spheres, I am laying my reputation on the line. What would happen to you or by your actions would reflect on me as well, Gonzague concluded.

— One last thing, Steve...you know perfectly well that flirting with the Odessa organization is very dangerous. The bullet in your shoulder is the proof that they can act irrationally if they feel they are in danger, Gonzague added.

— I realize perfectly well my situation in all this, and I realize that what I am asking you risks overflowing onto you and your reputation. Therefore, it has to be done in such a way that you can be easily exonerated, if something goes wrong, Steve stated.

— Steve, who are these five men? What are their names? I may know some of them. Gonzague asked.

— Their names are André Lemaitre, Rudolf Autord-Saulnier, Georges Du Val De Curzay, Jean-Marie Chapuit-Bouzerot, and Xavier Bonneliere, Steve replied.

— Steve, this reputation aspect is very important to me and I can see where you could go wrong on this, Gonzague explained.

— Georges Du Val De Curzay is not only a friend and associate in some of my industrial endeavors; I have known him almost since childhood school. We attended the same boarding school in Normandy called L'ecole des Roches from age eleven to fifteen. We have never lost contact since. So you see just how delicate this can be for me if you accuse someone falsely, concluded Gonzague.

— Gonzague, I am perfectly aware of the consequences of anything I could do, but you know me well enough to be sure that I would not make any moves without consulting you first, Steve said.

— This is great. You have already eliminated one so we only have four suspects now, Steve commented.

They discussed long into the evening and finally concluded that Gonzague would introduce Steve into the upper sphere, but only as a journalist.

— You are a very personable person and I do not think that once introduced, you can maintain your contacts alone, said Gonzague.

— We agree, Steve; you will make no accusations without first consulting me; I underline the importance of this point, Gonzague instructed.

— That is clearly and absolutely agreed upon, Gonzague, Steve agreed.

— Benedict, when will I have a social meeting with any of the remaining four men? Gonzague asked.

— I will check your agenda right now and hopefully all four can be met at the same time. If not, I will prepare a list of social events for Steve in which you and one or more of the four men will participate. In the worst case, I will email it to you, Steve, Benedict promised.

— Now that your problem is settled, when are you and your lovely wife Ping coming to stay with me for a week or more? Gonzague asked with a firm tone.

— Let us decide on that when this project is over. You know that both of us really do want to come. Ping speaks often of you, Steve concluded.

— I suggest that we retire now, I do have a very busy schedule tomorrow...and by the way, Steve, I am going to Paris Le Bourget first thing tomorrow, so if you want to join me, you are welcome, Gonzague offered.

— You can bet your bottom dollar I would like that; otherwise, I would waste the entire day in travel, Steve said.

— Benedict, you have my email and my cell phone number right? Steve asked.

— I certainly do, Steve...no problem there, Benedict assured.

They all retired after that and rose early to prepare for the coming day. Steve and Gonzague went to his private airport and they flew to Paris in about one hour's time.

Gonzague met a delegation of industrialists with whom he had important negotiations. Steve took the RER (regional express railway) from Le Bourget directly to the heart of Paris where he switched stations and got a metro to the station right next to his apartment.

Ping was out when Steve arrived so he got straight on to the Internet to gather as much information about each of the remaining four men, André Lemaitre, Rudolf Autord-Saulnier, Jean-Marie Chapuit-Bouzerot, and Xavier Bonneliere, as he could.

There were newspaper articles, and some sites even gave more personal information, such as their home and office addresses and phone numbers.

Steve was amazed at the amount of information a person could acquire on just anyone. It was understandable the amount of identity theft that had become a problem even in France these days.

Benedict was very timely and sent Gonzague's agenda. It showed that Gonzague had to participate in a fund raising cocktail/dinner for the annual SIDA (AIDS) fund drive.

André Lemaitre was also to be present and Benedict had arranged with the organizers to place Gonzague and Steve at the same table as André Lemaitre. It was to occur at six o'clock in the evening in three days. Benedict ensured that an invitation was sent to Steve because a person had to be invited to get into one of these affairs. Gonzague prepaid Steve's meal. Steve had money but Gonzague knew that he would have second thoughts about paying five thousand Euros for a meal.

The studies Steve had made about André Lemaitre showed that he was an avid bicycle fan and rider. He generally made the weekend run around the Bois de Boulogne.

The Bois de Boulogne is a park located along the western edge of the 16th arrondissement of Paris, near the suburb of Boulogne-Billancourt and Neuilly-sur-Seine. The Bois de Boulogne covers an area of 3.266 square miles, which is 2.5 times larger than Central Park in New York, and comparable in size to Richmond Park in London.

The Jardin d'Acclimatation occupies the northern part of the Bois de Boulogne. There is also an amusement park with a ménagerie and other attractions. The Bois de Boulogne is full of activities on the weekends. Such as biking, jogging, boat rowing, and remote control speedboats; picnics are allowed, but private barbeques are not allowed.

During summer season, the bois holds a three-day weekend party in the month of July with over fifty bands and singers. Mostly students that camp out overnight attend this.

Steve was aware of this bicycle tour of the Bois de Boulogne made by a group of more or less famous personalities. Steve knew that the most famous French TV sports caster and two French movie stars always made the weekend tour together when they were available in Paris. The group was composed of more than one hundred personalities and rich industrialists, so there were always enough persons present each weekend to make the tour.

Either the group would make a tour on the twenty-mile riding track or sixty miles of roadway; most of the participants were high-level amateurs.

Everyone met at the Longchamp Racecourse facility, which is a fifty-seven-hectare horseracing facility located on the Route des Tribunes in the Bois de Boulogne. This course hosts the racing season's most fashionable social event, the Prix de l'Arc de Triomphe.

The bicycle riders use the jockeys' locker rooms and showers since only a few arrive completely dressed in the traditional bicycle-racing outfit. Steve knew that this was his chance to approach André Lemaitre and especially have the chance to see his armpit in the showers.

It had been a while since he had ridden his bicycle. He enjoyed a pastime when he lived in the Paris suburbs. There were many paved cycling paths especially the one near his house, which followed the Marne River for eighteen miles almost to the limits of Paris.

Steve joined the fund raising cocktail at six o'clock as indicated and almost immediately sited Gonzague talking to two men. Gonzague saw him coming; he was never the one to hesitate.

— Steve, come here my friend, Gonzague called to him.

— Good evening gentlemen, my name is Steve Santa, semi-retired journalist and author, Steve said, as he shook hands with the three men, as was the custom in France.

— Steve, let me present Georges Bidault, senator from Paris 15th arrondissement...and do not believe a word he says. He is an expert politician and he is in the opposition, Gonzague said, while introducing a very tall and thin man Steve had seen in the TV news very often.

— This is Xavier Piquarde, general director of Piquarde Industries. Treat him well Steve, he is one of my associate, Gonzague mused, as he introduced the second man.

— Of course, you are the American journalist kidnapped in Dubna Russia with two Russian scientists. That must have been a terrible ordeal for you to live through, said Xavier.

— The Chechen rebels did not mistreat us at all and we were lucky enough to be rescued by the US forces in the area quickly. However, I will tell you I did have the scare of my life, Steve explained.

The conversations had started well and Steve felt more or less accepted in the company of these two important personalities, so he had good hopes for meeting André Lemaitre. The cocktail was ending and everyone was moving to the tables. Steve looked at the place cards to find his seat. Steve, Gonzague, Xavier, and Georges found their table; André Lemaitre was already seated. Introductions were made again because everyone did not necessarily know the others.

The master of ceremonies opened the session with a short speech and wished everyone to enjoy the meal. With that formality accomplished, the servers began to bring the start of the meal to the tables.

Xavier who was very curious about the details of Steve's Chechen ordeal led the conversation at the table. Steve was seated next to André so he addressed him often. Once Xavier's curiosity had been satisfied, Steve asked if they could talk about lighter subjects. It took some talking to direct the conversation to the subject of individual sports activities.

Once on the subject of personal sports activities everyone engaged in the conversation because it was not only fun, but also it was one of their stress eliminators. Luckily, André opened the subject of his bicycle tours on weekends with the group of personalities. As the conversation wore on, André seemed to have accepted Steve enough to invite him to come on one of their weekend adventures, with the warning that it was a grueling task to keep up with the platoon.

The conversation went to wine and each person gave his opinion on his favorite wine. André and Steve both like upper burgundy and especially Chablis. Steve was not only a specialist but also an authority on Chablis.

This drew the two men closer since they appreciated the same things. André and Steve exchanged business cards and André even wrote his private cell number for Steve. This was a proof of acceptance. Gonzague was a miracle worker.

As the evening ended, Steve walked out with Gonzague to his waiting car. He thanked him for masterminding this encounter and reassured him that nothing would be done without consulting him first. Steve was only on an investigative phase now.

Friday arrived quickly and Steve called André to see if he was going to participate that weekend. In fact, in acceptation into the platoon of bicycle riding personalities, could only be made by and introduction of an already accepted member who became his mentor. André was going to attend the Sunday session and they were to meet at eight o'clock Sunday morning at the jockeys' dressing room to suit up.

Steve was very excited at the aspect of running with the big guys, as he would say. Steve had gone to the local gym to exercise every day to be sure he would not look too foolish.

Steve took a taxi with his bike in the trunk. There was no traffic on Sunday, so he arrived quickly at the Longchamp Racecourse facility. The taxi was admitted and drove directly to the jockeys' dressing rooms. There were already a handful of cyclists, suited up and ready to go, in conversation at the front of the door.

Steve quickly got into the dressing room and suited up. This took time, as he had to put on cycling shorts and jersey. He also had the matching Windfront vest, gloves and hat. His cycling equipment was all "Livestrong," demonstrating his fidelity to the American cycling hero.

As soon as he was ready, he went outside where André was waiting with a few friends. André made the introductions and then said:

— We are all to meet at the Rue des Fortifications, just past the Porte de Passy, so let's get-going Steve, André said, as he mounted his superb bike and started slowly, waiting for Steve to get going.

They rode a grueling fifteen-mile ride on a flat surface mostly paved, but there was one stretch in cobblestones where you had to be very careful to avoid falling. After the first ten minutes, Steve's leg muscles were crying out for air. They hurt so badly because the pace the platoon had taken was rather fast.

Nevertheless, Steve was adamant, he wanted to make a descent showing and not become a straggler, so he pumped on using all the force he had. *Good thing I ate my Wheaties this morning,* Steve thought, as he strained to peddle with the rest of the platoon.

Happily, the platoon stopped after the first complete tour to water-up and relax their muscles a little. The pause was southing to Steve, and walking around a little made his aching leg muscles feel better. However, before he could really feel reinvigorated, the platoon saddled up and was off at the frantic pace they had held throughout the tour.

Off he went, but this time his leg muscles started giving more strength and he could stay abreast of André. This time they were able to talk a bit as they peddled. Steve opened the subject of Chablis and they had a few exchanges.

Steve could not be happier than when they arrived back at the Longchamp Racecourse facility. After a short talk in front of the jockeys' locker room about how the tour went, the group started dispersing, some to their cars, others taking off again on their bicycles headed home, and André, Steve, and a whole group headed for the showers and dressing rooms.

Steve kept the conversation going on the Chablis subject because he figured that it would allow him to remain close enough to see André's armpit when they hit the shower. Effectively, they did shower together and Steve did get to see André's left armpit and there was nothing, nothing. Well, at least this eliminated André as being the last escapee, three more to go, Steve was thinking as he dressed.

Steve stayed a moment and talked with some of the other participants, while André was in a hurry to return home. The other members were sympathetic to Steve's arrival in their midst and encouraged him to come back and ride with them often. Steve finally called a taxi and returned to his Montparnasse apartment.

Steve put his bicycle away in the basement, went up to the apartment, and flopped into the first available chair. Ping could not stop teasing him about being an old man.

Steve chose Jean-Marie Chapuit-Bouzerot as the next person to investigate. He asked Benedict what information he had on Jean-Marie Chapuit-Bouzerot.

The response was surprising because Jean-Marie Chapuit-Bouzerot seemed to fit the description of a Front National member. He was Catholic but part of the dissident Roman Catholic Church that had made a scission from Rome when the mass liturgy was changed from Latin to the local language. He was also present at the traditional Joan of Arc feast day ceremony in front of her statue Place des Pyramides, just opposite the Louvre Pyramid.

As far as Benedict could gather from the press and other sources, Jean-Marie was not officially a member of the Front National, but then the Front National was so secretive about its members and especially its political contributors that it would take a subpoena to get the real information.

Steve started Googling Jean-Marie Chapuit-Bouzerot to see what he could find himself. He was the executive vice president for Strategic Initiatives and Partnerships in the French telecom company.

He had attended "Ecole nationale des Arts et Métiers d'Aix-en-Provence" and "Ecole nationale supérieure des Telecommunications de Paris" and had worked in other large communications companies in France.

Everything seemed to be normal about him. Steve could even trace him right back to when he was in college at eighteen years old. Even the photos of him then gave rise to believe that it was the same morphology of the man sixty-three years old today. Steve was stumped as to how he could check this man's armpit. It seemed that he had no sporting activity other than being an avid casting angler.

Steve decided to leave Jean-Marie Chapuit-Bouzerot for the moment and concentrate on Rudolf Autord-Saulnier.

Rudolf Autord-Saulnier was the owner of a large cooperative farming industry near Cavaillion, which produced most of France's melons as well as other small fruits. These cooperative farms and the collection centers were located in the Vaucluse department just fifty miles north of Marseilles.

Here again, Steve was stumped by the fact that he could trace Rudolf Autord-Saulnier's history and even his family history back three or four generations and he had brothers and sisters so this would eliminate him definitely as one of the escapees.

This left only Xavier Bonneliere to investigate. His family was known for producing Chinon wine. The vineyards are located in the Vienne River in the heart of the Loire valley area. Internet gathered history indicated that the chateau and its vineyards were falling into ruins until Xavier Bonneliere returned from South America with seemingly a large personal fortune.

Although another family by the name of Blanchard owned the chateau, Xavier Bonneliere bought into the chateau and invested to make it one of the most well known wines in the area.

Return from South America, large personal fortune, this has to be my man, thought Steve.

Steve was back in touch with Benedict to find out if he had any other information, but Benedict could only confirm what Steve had already found. However, the questions remained about where he had lived in South America and his fortune came from.

Xavier Bonneliere had effectively left France in 1947 after the war because there was no work and his family had been complete annihilated during the war. He did not have even one living relative, so he decided to move on and make a new life in a new and rich country like Argentina.

Upon arriving in Buenos Aires in 1947, he had no problem finding what could be done because he spoke very good Spanish. He met a rich Argentinean cattle farmer who was looking for a foreman and who saw in Xavier Bonneliere a man with a solid determination and strong personality.

This man hired Xavier Bonneliere, but in a few years, Xavier had learned about the sheep raising growth in Patagonia around a city named Rio Gallegos. Xavier worked hard and his Argentinean mentor paid him well. He had saved enough to buy a small farm he wanted to use for growing sheep. He was in on the first wave of investors in sheep raising in the area.

As the years went by, Xavier and two other sheep ranchers built the first slaughterhouse in Rio Gallegos. The next years brought about a large growth in the demand for wool, mainly by the US and China. This brought about a rapid expansion of his activities so his fortune came from raising sheep.

About half of Argentina's fifteen million sheep are in Patagonia, because of the investment in the slaughterhouses in Rio Gallegos at the southernmost tip of Argentina. Xavier Bonneliere owned a quarter of all sheep-raising activities in Patagonia before selling out and returning to France.

Steve got to tracing Xavier Bonneliere's records on the Internet and with the French authorities.

Finally, after exhausting almost all of the resources searching for Xavier Bonneliere, Steve asked for an appointment at the National Veterans and War Victims (ONACVG) Administration that was part of the Department of Defense.

After entering into the dark and solemn building and checking in at the reception desk. A man came out and asked Steve to follow him. They went to his office where Steve explained that he was doing an article on the survivors of the French SS Charlemagne division and needed to identify a person.

The man got on his PC and started a search on the name Xavier Bonneliere, because if he was in the system that would mean that he was never a member of the French SS Charlemagne division. The system manages all aspects of veteran's lives in the same manner as the VA in the US.

After a few minutes, up came a record on his screen concerning Xavier Bonneliere. He was demobilized in 1946. He joined the French Forces of the Interior (FFI) and his unit was incorporated into the Gaullist "Army of the Rhine and Danube" until his demobilization in November 1946, he served in the French occupation of Germany.

This was all the man could tell Steve, but it confirmed that Xavier Bonneliere was not the last escapee; he was truly a French soldier and could not have participated in the French SS Charlemagne division.

As Steve left on his way back to the apartment, he could not stop thinking that is should have been this man. He fit the description completely, but he had to yield to the military records in the French administration.

Back at the apartment, Steve and Ping discussed this setback. They had been through all five men likely to be the last escapee and none seemed to fit.

—   In fact, Ping, two persons are doubtful. One is Xavier Bonneliere and the other is Jean-Marie

Chapuit-Bouzerot, who seems to be a Front National sympathizer.

— The background check you made on Jean-Marie Chapuit-Bouzerot was very thorough and there was proof of continuity of his family and his life so I do not think it can be him, Ping said.

— I have a tendency to think like you, Ping. However, if it is Xavier Bonneliere, what can we do—follow him around every day and see where he goes and what he does? Steve proposed.

— That would be an impossible task, Ping, you and I are just not enough manpower to accomplish that sort of mission, Steve concluded.

— Steve, I have the solution, but I must go talk to someone in Chinatown, Ping suggested.

— We have many Chinese friends there in the 13th and 14th arrondissements of Paris. If I ask, I am sure that they would be willing to help us. They are very organized you know, Ping said.

— OK, Ping; I think you have a super idea there, but we will have to follow Xavier Bonneliere day and night and no matter where he goes, except abroad of course, Steve agreed.

216

— I will go and see them this afternoon, Steve, Ping concluded.

— Ping, please tell them that in all cases, they are not to contact him or try to follow him into a place where they are not allowed like a private home or something like that, Steve instructed.

— I understand, Steve; we just want to know everywhere he goes and when, right? Ping affirmed.

— It would be good if they could give us a report each night, too so we can record everything, Steve concluded.

That afternoon Ping went to see Huang Po Sin, her Wing Chun master and owner of the local exercise gym for specialists. Po Sin was also the local Jinrong (ancient Chinese title used to address high officials).

Ping explained what she and Steve wanted, and Po Sin agreed to help them. He would send out squads of his cong shu (handymen) on motorbikes to follow this Xavier Bonneliere and note the times and places he goes to.

This went on for more than two weeks and Steve and Ping scrupulously noted all of the comings and goings of Xavier Bonneliere. Obviously, the comings and goings were more or less standard. Almost every day, at a given hour, you could almost predict where

217

he would be. Steve knew that when statistics are too repetitive, you must look only at the exceptions.

The only exception in two weeks was a one-hour stopover at a gentleman's club in the 16th arrondissement, Place Victor Hugo. Steve asked Ping to tell Po Sin to have his men note everyone who entered the gentleman's club and even take cell phone photos of them without being observed.

With the mass of information they had collected, Steve and Ping suspected that there was some sort of meeting place that was on a personal level. It could be nothing, or it could have something to do with his status with respect to Odessa, if he were the last escapee.

Steve and Ping arrange all the information into a catalogue of addresses, times, and photos. Then Steve contacted Gonzague to tell him that he would like to get help from a Jewish organization specializing in the pursuit and capture of ex-Nazis.

Gonzague, however, insists that Steve take the case information to an informal contact in the French DST (Directorate of Territorial Surveillance).

There were four major missions of the DST:

❖ Surveillance of the Muslim World and Counter-terrorism Division

- ❖ Security, Heritage Protection, and Proliferation Division,

- ❖ Counter-espionage Division,

- ❖ Technical and Computer Services Division.

Gonzague had a friend in which he had perfect confidence in the Security, Heritage Protection and Proliferation Division. He wanted Steve to meet with the person who had also participated in the research for ex-Nazis and treasures lost during World War II. His name was Thibault Chedron de Courcel. Gonzague had arranged a meeting at the famous café on the Boulevard Sainte Germain called "Les Deux Magots." This was one of the most famous meeting places of the resistance members and later public figures such as Ernest Hemingway, Jean-Paul Sartre, and Simone de Beauvoir, and even Pablo Picasso.

— Do not worry Steve, he will recognize you as you enter inside the restaurant and move toward the left, near the bay windows. Thibault is in his sixties, has all gray hair, and wears glasses. I have sent him your photo so there should be no problem, Gonzague said.

— Steve you may talk to this man as if you were talking to me. I have perfect confidence in him and his judgment. Please abide by his advice and obey to the letter everything he tells you to do. This is of the strictest importance, Steve, and you know me so you know what this means, Gonzague commanded Steve, with a most serious tone of voice.

— You have my full agreement, Gonzague, Steve promised.

Steve met with Thibault at the appointed time and found a man who was rather sympathetic, but who conducted himself as if he was aware of every minute detail of all things around him. Steve explained the adventures he and Ping had gone through up to now and all the dangers they had confronted to find the escapees and perhaps the rest of the lost Stechovice treasure. Thibault listened carefully to everything Steve said without interrupting. When Steve had finished, Thibault engaged the conversation.

— Steve...I may call you Steve, right. I am very surprised at the work you have accomplished in this project. Even the best of my men would have had little success in doing what you and your wife have accomplished, Thibault said.

— Now you have come to the last, perhaps most important phase, which is final, and certain identification of Xavier Bonneliere, who may in reality be Kurt Bischwiller, Thibault said.

— Now, Steve, what I am going to tell you is of the strictest top secret. Our mutual friend Gonzague has perfect confidence and I can see

220

where your loyalties are through all of your actions, Thibault went on.

— We have been searching for the modern day Odessa organization too. Of course, we know of its existence, but we do not have any proof. You may just be supplying us with that proof. By the way, we have noticed a sudden increase of interest by Chinese people in the gentleman's club Place Victor Hugo. Do you have anything to do with this? Thibault asked.

— Yes, Thibault, my wife Ping has friends in the Chinese community, in the 13th and 14th arrondissements. Her contacts there were nice enough to provide scouting work for us by following Xavier Bonneliere everywhere and feeding the information back to us in order to construct this document, Steve said.

— Steve, with what I and my services know, combined with the information you are giving me, I am sure that we have pinpointed the location of the modern day Odessa organization, Thibault said in a very low-key tone, while he cupped his hand partially around his mouth to avoid any lip reading.

Thibault told Steve that they were going to make a raid on the gentleman's club Place Victor Hugo and they would wait to do it until Xavier Bonneliere was physically present.

221

He instructed Steve to stop all investigations until this operation was over. Furthermore, Thibault insisted that Steve and Ping be present at the raid. They were to stay outside of the club until the operation was over. However, he did want Steve and Ping to have the credit of having contributed to the capture and dismantling of the modern Odessa organization. Steve was to be present after the capture of Xavier Bonneliere when they would verify if he had the tattoo or scar under the left armpit.

Steve thanked him and asked if Gonzague approved, because he had a promise to keep with Gonzague, to which Thibault smiled and assured Steve that it was cleared.

Steve would be notified to come at a moment's notice because there was no way for them to plan the random movements of Xavier Bonneliere to be sure he was in the club when they raided it.

On the third day after Steve's meeting with Thibault, he received a call telling him to get to the place Victor Hugo immediately.

> — Come on Ping. They are going the gentleman's club in a few minutes and we should be there when the raid has finished so they can confront Xavier Bonneliere, shouted Steve with an excited voice.

They took the metro which was the quickest way of getting anywhere in Paris and arrived to see men from the DST as well as many Paris police, and even a company of CRS, the French riot police. Steve identified himself to the officer who seemed to be in charge, so that he could notify Thibault that he and Ping were present.

Steve and Ping were told to wait because important investigations were being carried out right then and no one could be admitted until it was finished.

Just as the press and television personnel started arriving, Steve saw Thibault come out and indicate to the officer that Steve and Ping could come into the building.

As Steve and Ping entered, they saw a few persons handcuffed and waiting to one side. Thibault came to meet Steve and Ping.

— So this is your beautiful wife Gonzague has told me about. I am charmed to meet you Mrs. Santa, Thibault greeted, and in traditional French style, in spite of the circumstances.

— Please come with me now to the office over there. We have Xavier Bonneliere there now and we are interrogating him as to his presence here, Thibault explained.

As they entered into the room, the DST men moved away to give access to Thibault. Steve and Ping were ordered to one side while Thibault proceeded to interrogate Xavier Bonneliere.

— Monsieur Bonneliere, I want you to remove you coat and shirt, Thibault demanded. It was an order and a request.

— You cannot do this to me. I will have you kicked out of the DST for this embarrassment. You are not a gentleman, Monsieur. Anyway, why do you want to see my bare chest? Xavier Bonneliere asked in protest.

— Just do as I say, Thibault said with a commanding tone of voice, almost expressing anger.

Xavier Bonneliere started removing his tie and suit coat. He hesitated like for a moment until Thibault told him to get the shirt off too. Xavier Bonneliere took off his shirt and undershirt as well and then a DTS man went next to him and raised his left arm.

There was no tattoo, but there was a large scare indicating that something was removed.

— I accuse you of being Kurt Bischwiller living here illegally under the name of Xavier Bonneliere. You under arrest for this and for reselling part of the Stechovice treasure, that was part of the SS war loot. There is no prescription for this crime, said Thibault. The words shot out of his mouth like thunderbolts, judging by the reaction of Kurt Bischwiller.

As he was hand cuffed and taken out to the polite van, Thibault shook Steve's hand, but gave the four traditional French cheek kisses to Ping.

— When we have finished our dossier on this man, we must absolutely have dinner some time, Thibault said with enthusiasm.

— We would love that Thibault, Ping and Steve said together, with a large smile.

— Steve, I believe you still have one more action to accomplish right. Thibault asked.

— Just as soon as I get back to the apartment I will get the email off to some surprised people, Steve promised.

When Steve and Ping arrived at the apartment, Steve got onto the Internet and sent an email to the Monuments Men Foundation for the Preservation of Art in Dallas, Texas.

He explained the whereabouts of the remainder of the treasure in Peru and the capture of the last escapee of the missing French SS Charlemagne Division squad and the money Kurt Bischwiller had in his care, which was part of the Stechovice treasure.

When the email was finished, Steve and Ping sat on the couch close to each other and talked about what had happened to them.

— You know, Steve, in the past, when we have finished a project like this, we generally go on vacation somewhere nice. I have a terrific proposal to make this time. Do you want to hear it? Ping asked.

— Of course, darling, I know you generally have the best ideas. What is it? Where should we go this time? Steve asked, anxious to receive her suggestion.

— Steve darling, I propose that we stay here in the apartment and do not go anywhere for a week, not even for food or to meet anyone. This has been so dangerous that I want to have you all to myself for at least this one week, Ping announced.

"Chiche" was the only word Steve said, as he took her into his arms and kissed her tenderly.

Printed in Great Britain
by Amazon

60914524R00131